Bad Deal in Buckskin

Two unemployed wranglers are given a gold nugget for helping an old prospector named Huggy Johnson, whose wagon has broken down. Alamo Todd Heffridge and his partner Kid Streater unwittingly sell the nugget to an unscrupulous assay agent in the Arizona town of Buckskin. When Huggy is shot dead over a map which pin-points the location of the infamous Lost Dutchman Mine, the two wranglers are accused of the crime and arrested.

Can they escape from jail and find the real killers? Their fate lies in the hands of a saloon madame called Galloping Jane who is sweet on the Kid. But all does not go according to plan…. Bullets are sure to fly and blood sure to spill before the Dutchman's long lost secret is revealed.

By the same author

Dead Man Walking
Two for Texas
Divided Loyalties
Return of the Gunfighter
Dynamite Daze
Apache Rifles
Duel at Del Norte
Outlaw Queen
When Lightning Strikes
Praise Be to Silver
A Necktie for Gifford
Navajo Sunrise
Shotgun Charade
Blackjacks of Nevada
Derby John's Alibi
Long Ride to Purgatory
No Way Back
Revenge Burns Deep

Writing as Dale Graham
High Plains Vendetta
Dance with the Devil
Nugget!
Montezuma's Legacy
Death Rides Alone
Gambler's Dawn
Vengeance at Bittersweet
Justice for Crockett
Bluecoat Renegade
Gunsmoke over New Mexico
Montaine's Revenge
Black Gold
Backshooter
Bitter Trail
The Restless Gun
Snake Eyes
Sundown Over the Sierras
Wyoming Blood Feud
Hangman's Reach

Bad Deal at Buckskin

Ethan Flagg

A Black Horse Western
ROBERT HALE

ISBN 978-0-7198-1916-2

The Crowood Press
The Stable Block
Crowood Lane
Ramsbury
Marlborough
Wiltshire SN8 2HR

www.crowood.com

Robert Hale is an imprint
of The Crowood Press

Typeset by Catherine Williams, Knebworth

Printed and bound in Great Britain by
CPI Group (UK) Ltd, Croydon CR0 4YY

ONE

A HELPING HAND

It was a fine sunny morning in early May. A brief flurry of rain overnight had encouraged plants to flower. The desert had come alive. Red blooms of ocotillo and strawberry cactus vied for pride of place with golden columbine. Birds were singing merrily. Even a desert rat, normally a nocturnal creature, had come out of its lair to enjoy the delights of spring.

All things considered, the two riders nudging their mounts across the open flats of the Papago Rim ought likewise to have been savouring these scintillating bounties of nature. Yet whereas bright sunlight lit up the plateau lands, and cactus wrens twittered, a cloud hung over these two itinerant wranglers. Not even the comical antics of a roadrunner shooting across their path enunciating its familiar *beep beep*, could raise a smile.

Todd Heffridge, known as Alamo, hooked out the makings from his vest pocket. It was a listless action. A morose look impaired his ruggedly handsome features. Single-handedly, he rolled a couple of stogies, handing one to his partner.

Kid Streater accepted it without comment. His own gloomy expression strove to rival that of his buddy. Older than his pard by ten years, Streater had acquired his youthful nickname due to his stocky build and trusting nature. Less admirable critters who sought to take advantage of the Kid's affability had paid the price with bloodied noses. Yet there were few cowpunchers who could outclass Streater when it came to taming wild mustangs. He was able to read the equine mind like no other jasper Alamo had ever met.

Both men lit up and puffed lazily.

'That's the last of the tobacco,' grunted the younger man, tossing aside the empty sack. His left hand strayed to the saddle bag strapped behind the cantle. 'And we ain't exactly well stocked up with grub. Three sticks of beef jerky and a couple of apples won't sustain us for long.'

Nearby a coyote sat perched on a ledge of rock, howling at the sun.

'That critter is likely to enjoy a better midday meal than us,' complained Streater. A disconsolate twist of the lip was aimed at his partner. 'If'n you had kept your durned hands off'n the boss's wife, we wouldn't be in this mess. It was only by the skin of our teeth that we escaped with our hides intact.'

Alamo responded with his own scratchy rejoinder. 'Ugh! You slugging it out with the foreman didn't do us any favours, neither. You should have kept them mitts safely in your pockets. Tangling with Butch Addison was a bum move that's gotten us into this durned pickle.'

'The damned asshole shouldn't have accused me of letting him ride that bay mare afore it was properly broke in.' The Kid huffed and puffed, squaring his stocky frame. 'I told him not to mount up until I'd checked her myself. But would he listen? That clown don't know one end of a cayuse from the other. Served the idiot right when that bronc tossed him into the dirt.'

'You didn't help yourself by creasing up with laughter like a braying jackass,' chided Alamo, blowing a perfect smoke ring. Although he couldn't resist a sly smirk at the recollection of seeing the arrogant foreman grovelling in the dust.

'At least the gal I was courting didn't have a husband,' Streater snapped back, drawing hard on the wafer thin stogie. 'I was making good progress with Molly Bender before you went and put the kibosh on things. Now we've had to skip the valley and hope those jaspers don't pick up our trail.'

Alamo sighed. 'That lunkhead of a rancher didn't deserve a dame like Sarah. He couldn't give her what I could.'

A twinkle in his eye elicited a mordant grunt from his partner. 'Talk about me keeping my hands in my pockets,' the older wrangler hooted. 'You, old buddy, should have kept your—'

'OK, Kid, I get the message,' Alamo cut him short.

'Guess we both let our natural instincts overrule our heads.'

'And look where it's gotten us.'

Silence descended over the two buddies as they both settled back into contemplating a future that was decidedly uncertain. No job and they had been forced to skedaddle sharpish from the Longhorn Ranch in Arizona's San Dimitri Valley. Being sent packing was a harsh blow to their self-esteem. A brash lesson that did not sit well with two experienced cowhands.

They paused at the top of a rise to scan their back trail.

'At least we seem to have got away safely,' was Alamo's pertinent observation. 'There's nobody tailing us.'

The self-imposed getaway was made all the more irksome knowing they were only two days off the monthly payout. And on this occasion the boss had promised the whole crew a bonus in their pay packets. So no wages, and no grub, neither.

Both men huddled further into their sheepskin coats to stave off the early morning chill. Dour expressions informed a watching line of bluebirds that their future looked decidedly bleak.

'Look on the bright side, Kid,' Alamo commented as they drew rein. He pointed to a sign board nailed to a cottonwood. 'At least now we're out of Gila County. So we can look for work on another spread. Good wranglers are always needed.'

'You'd better pray that the boss man don't wire the other ranchers in the territory to keep a lookout for us.'

The younger man threw him a startled look of concern. 'He wouldn't do that ... would he?'

The Kid shrugged. 'Who knows? But if'n we are in the clear, you just remember next place we sign on to keep away from the boss's wife.'

The reprimand provoked a bashful smirk from the recipient before Alamo countered with his own caustic rejoinder. 'And you keep that temper of your'n in check when the foreman hands out orders.'

Sometime later they crested a low rise and came upon a wagon drawn by two horses. It was stuck fast and leaning at an ungainly angle. One of the back wheels had broken and the owner was struggling to raise the axle to fit a spare. But it was an impossible task for an old dude travelling on his ownsome.

'Looks like that jigger is in need of our help, Kid,' urged Alamo, spurring down the shallow grade. Streater followed close behind.

The sweating traveller was so engrossed in his hopeless task that he failed to heed the approach of the two wranglers. Only when they drew to a halt beside him did he suddenly realize he was not alone. A hand grabbed for the old Springfield rifle resting close at hand.

'Easy there, old timer,' Alamo cautioned, raising his hands to show they meant him no harm. 'We were just passing and saw that you were in trouble. You ain't gonna get that fixed by plugging us.'

The old guy relaxed. He took off a shapeless hat. A shock of iron grey hair matched the drooping moustache that twitched irritably.

'You sure ain't wrong there, stranger,' he grumbled. 'The back wheel fell into a rut and broke on that rock.' He slung a finger towards the offending culprit. A grubby bandanna stroked away the gritty sweat from a face boasting more lines than a dime novel. 'I should have changed it weeks ago. But I've been too busy working my claim.'

'You a miner?' enquired Streater, dismounting to take a closer look at the damage.

The guy nodded. 'Been prospecting in these parts for nigh on two years. Never had much luck until recently. I was heading for the county seat at Phoenix to stake my claim when this happened. The last five hours have been sheer hell.' He slumped down, resting his back against the broken wheel. 'And I'm plumb tuckered.'

'My name's Todd Heffridge. Some folks call me Alamo,' the young wrangler said before introducing his buddy. 'And this is my partner, Kid Streater. We're wranglers looking for work.'

'Huggy Johnson,' said the miner, holding out a hand. They all shook. 'It's a stroke of luck you fellas coming along. Otherwise I'd have been forced to leave the wagon and ride bare-back to the nearest town.' He rubbed the seat of his pants. 'I sure ain't no durned redskin.'

'You rest up for spell, Huggy. Me and the Kid will soon have this sorted out,' Alamo assured the exhausted miner.

'Kid Streater, you say? Your buddy don't exactly look in the first flush of youth,' the miner said with a frown. 'He up to some hard graft?'

'Don't worry, old timer,' Alamo grinned. 'He just looks older than he is. A loco mustang he was trying to break aged him ten years when it objected to his busting technique. Turned the poor sucker grey overnight.'

'You believe that hogwash, mister, you'll believe anything,' remarked a jaundiced Streater, accepting the jocular teasing in good part. Nevertheless he was ready with his own piece of erudite wisdom. 'They call him Alamo cos he don't know when to quit. Stubborn as an ornery jackass and twice as ugly.'

'Guess that makes us even,' conceded his partner.

The two men then set to work with a will. It was a hot day so they both stripped off their vests and shirts. First off they had to empty the wagon of all the gear stowed inside to lighten the load. Next they took hold of the pit prop with which Johnson had been vainly trying to raise it. The combined strength of both men was required to lift the heavy wagon. It was a weighty beast. Slowly but surely they managed to raise it sufficiently to support the back axle with some boxes.

With Alamo exerting his whole body strength to hold the wagon in position, Streater was able to slacken the bolts securing the broken wheel and remove it. Both men were soon sweating, breathing hard and panting heavily with the severe exertion. The Kid daubed a wedge of grease onto the new hub before sliding the spare wheel onto the end connecting rod of the axle. He then proceeded to tighten up the locking pin.

'Hurry it up, Kid,' Alamo gasped out. His whole body

11

was trembling with the strain. 'My arms feel like they're being pulled out the sockets.'

'Quit your griping, boy,' Streater mocked his pal, eager to get his own back for the recent ribbing at his expense. 'You're allus flexing them muscles to show the local gals how tough you are. Now prove you got the makings.' Streater's grin was wider than the Rio Grande as he continued to rag his friend. Finally he let the younger man off the hook. 'OK, you can lower it now. But keep it slow and steady.'

Wheezing like an old steam engine, Todd Heffridge slumped to the ground. He was bushed. Johnson handed them a full water bottle each, the contents of which were drained at one go. 'Reckon you boys deserve some'n a mite stronger after all that effort,' he said as the two labourers recovered their breath.

The bottle of Scotch whiskey produced by the miner cracked a sweat-beaded grin of approval on Streater's face.

'Now that's more like it,' the Kid snorted, tipping the bottle and imbibing a hefty slug. 'Aaaaah!' he sighed. 'Just what the doctor ordered. That sure is good stuff, Huggy.' Another gulp soon followed. Alamo was content with the water. Truth be told, he was more of a beer-drinking man.

The old prospector smiled. 'You keep the bottle. I got three more in the wagon.'

The Kid's eyes lit up. 'That's mighty generous, Huggy. You certain you want to give away good whiskey?'

The miner shrugged. 'Least I can do after you boys helped me out of this tight spot,' the old miner enthused gratefully. 'I'm beholden to you. Don't bear thinking on what would have happened if'n you hadn't moseyed along. This route is way off the main trail. You are the first guys I've seen in over two months.'

He stood up and climbed into the wagon, appearing a minute later with a small burlap sack. Opening up the draw string, he removed a nugget of gold and handed it to Todd Heffridge. 'This little chunk ought to keep the wolf from the door until you boys find work.'

Both men gaped wide at the glinting yellow of the precious metal. It was of a rough knobbly appearance but no less alluring for that. Gold had that effect. It mesmerises all who behold its hypnotic attraction. A magic spell, the yellow peril is like a spider drawing the unwary into its potent grasp.

The two innocent wranglers were no different. They were well and truly hooked, landed and netted by the gold nugget's powerful embrace. Even though neither had any experience of placer mining, they could see it was a decent piece of hardware.

'You don't have to hand over your goods to us, Huggy,' the young wrangler burbled gently, handling the ugly hunk like it were a chick fresh from the egg. 'All we did was change a wheel.'

'I'm a firm believer in rewarding those who do me a good turn, boys,' Johnson insisted. 'If'n anybody deserves it, you do. And I've had some good luck with my present venture. That's why I want to register it. Having an official claim certificate will make me the legal owner.'

After so much arduous work, they decided to rest up and start off again the next morning. But first, Alamo had the miner ride up the trail aways to check the new wheel was securely in place.

'Good as new,' hollered Johnson gleefully on his return. 'Guess you boys could do with some grub after all that effort.'

The two wranglers were not about to deny that their stomachs were rumbling louder than a mountain avalanche. Shadows of late afternoon were creeping across the harsh terrain so they decided to camp out for the night with their benefactor. The miner was able to make them a meal of frijoles, rice and cornbread washed down with strong coffee laced with more Scotch. It was the first proper meal they had eaten since fleeing from the wrath of Longhorn ranch boss Howard Tomlin and his surly foreman.

It was a highly contented trio that settled down for the night amidst the raw beauty of Arizona's Mescal Range. Beyond the flickering embers of the fire, night creatures began their ritual calling. Owls hooted and coyotes howled. But good food and the soporific effect of the whiskey soon found them slumbering like new born babies. Not even the low growling of a mountain lion could disturb them.

TWO

A CUNNING FOX

The three associates set off next morning at first light. The town of Buckskin was less than a day's ride to the west.

'Seems like as good a place as any for you boys to find work,' Johnson said. 'And I'm hoping to meet my daughter off the stage tomorrow. I sent her a letter about the mine. She's coming out from Santa Fe to help me after we've registered it.'

'Is there an assay agent in Buckskin for us to cash in the nugget?' asked Streater.

Johnston's detached look told him the old guy did not have the answer the two men sought. 'I ain't visited the place afore,' he added. 'Any goods I need have been bought on the far side of the Mescals in Globe. Only reason I'm headed that way now is to register my claim and meet the stage.'

'Buckskin you say? Never heard of it,' said Streater.

'It sounds like a place where deer hunters might gather,' Alamo suggested as they trotted along.

'That will have been the case when those fellas only wore homemade gear,' agreed the miner. 'But those days are long gone. There are still plenty of mule deer in these parts. But times move on. Most folks prefer store-bought duds now.'

'You seem mighty clued-up, Huggy,' remarked an impressed Kid Streater.

'I was a hunting man myself for a spell up north in Colorado during the glory days of the trapping boom in the thirties.' Huggy Johnson's eyes misted over at the recollection. 'We were after beaver in those days. Jeepers! Them there rendezvous up on the Green River were some'n else, boys. We sure had us a rare old time.' He shrugged his bony shoulders. 'But all good things come to an end. The beaver got trapped. And I got married and had to settle down. I did some buffalo hunting for the army then took up as a wagon train scout before coming down here to try my hand at prospecting. That was when the gold bug bit me on the ass.'

'You sure have been around, old timer,' said Streater somewhat morosely. 'All I've ever done is work on ranches. Taming horses and pushing cattle up the trails to the Kansas railheads.'

'Don't run yourself down, Kid,' admonished the older man, wagging a reproachful finger at his benefactor. 'Everybody needs good beef. Cow-punching has always been a noble profession. And nobody can do that without well-trained horses.'

That positive comment perked Streater up. He nodded. 'Guess you're right there, Huggy. Only trouble is, I have a tendency to resent taking orders from simple-minded hard cases employed for their gun slinging ability more than any ranching skills.'

He was thinking of the recent spat with Butch Addison, the so-called foreman of the Longhorn. Him and a couple of other hired guns had been brought in especially to bolster Tomlin's ambition to take over the San Dimitri Valley. Once again the Kid's face dropped, his lip curling beneath the bushy side whiskers.

Alamo quickly filled the miner in on their sudden departure from the ranch and flight west. He tried avoiding his own lascivious indiscretions with Sarah Tomlin. But Streater soon put the record straight. The telling raised a hoot of laughter from the old miner.

'You ain't the only one to find himself scrambling out of a bedroom window in double quick time, boy. And you won't be the last.'

'Guess we won't be working in Gila County anymore,' added Alamo.

'Plenty of work further west for good cow hands,' replied Johnson. 'You guys will have no trouble getting signed on with the spring round-up under way. If'n you do have trouble, I can always give you some pick-and-shovel work on my claim to tide you over.'

'That's mighty obliging of you, Huggy,' said Alamo. 'We might well need to take you up on that.'

*

On reaching the small settlement of Buckskin, Huggy Johnson bid farewell to his companions. 'Figure I'll bunk down at the livery stable until my daughter arrives. The National Hotel is over yonder for you fellas when you've cashed in that nugget. I can never get used to those soft feather beds after months sleeping on hard ground. But you fellas enjoy yourselves. See ya around.'

The old miner waved a hand. It was reciprocated with gratitude. Then he slapped the leathers, moving off down to the far end of the street where the liveries were always located. Regular storekeepers objected to the smell of manure and sweating horseflesh that hung over such establishments.

'Reckon our first job is to do just like the man says and cash in this piece of good fortune,' Alamo said, hooking out the glittering lump. They both studied it closely. This was the first such item either man had ever set eyes on.

'How much do you think it's worth?' asked the bedazzled Kid.

'Not a clue,' replied his partner. 'Guess we'll have to trust the assay agent and accept whatever he is prepared to offer us.'

They nudged their mounts along the street, eyes searching for a signboard advertising the services of just such a trader.

Kid Streater's eyes meanwhile had been drawn to the proliferation of saloons in the small berg. Names like the Dancing Queen, Black Pig, Shady Lady and Rim Rock had the guy drooling at the thought of all that booze, not to mention dames. But mainly it was the chance to join a real poker game. Judging by the noise bursting through the open doorway, it was the Rim Rock that seemed to be offering the best action. And that piece of metal was his ticket to the high life.

There was only one metal assayer in Buckskin. It was run by a dude called Jonas Gribble. They pulled over and tied up outside the office.

No time was wasted in pushing through the door into the gloomy interior. The proprietor was carefully weighing some gold dust on a set of scales. He ignored the newcomers, concentrating all his attention on ensuring the pans were level before noting down the weight and value in a heavy black ledger.

The plank walls of the office were lined with photographs of grinning miners posing outside their claims. These were the lucky ones who were more than happy to shout their success to the world. Assay agents were always eager to display these jubilant few. It was good for business. Less was said of the many thousands more who were destined to grub out their lives for a pittance.

Shutting the thick tome, Jonas Gribble eyed the newcomers with that superior arrogance common to traders who knew they had the whip hand. The black toothbrush moustache twitched. Otherwise, he exuded an all-encompassing obsequious propriety.

'What can I do for you, gents?' he asked, rubbing his hands expectantly.

'We need you to value this gold nugget that's come our way,' said Alamo innocently, handing over the yellow lump of hard core.

It was fortunate for the agent that his premises were dimly illuminated. Jonas Gribble's Adam's apple bobbed in his throat. He was not called Foxy for nothing. Close set beady eyes greedily devoured the high quality of the precious metal. Straight away he perceived that this was no ordinary nugget. Under normal circumstances, he would not have enquired how a man came by his paydirt. It was immaterial, a guy's own business. All he usually wanted was to determine the ore content of what was being offered. But this piece was something special.

Gingerly he posed the question uppermost in his mind. 'Mind telling me how you came by this piece?' he enquired tentatively, trying to prevent the tremulous query sounding over-excited.

Alamo was not put out. Helping a fellow traveller and being rewarded was nothing to hide. 'We helped an old prospector on the trail whose wagon had broken down. This was his reward.'

Gribble dearly wanted to ask where the guy was at this moment without being inquisitive. But he needn't have worried. Kid Streater quickly filled in the gaps. 'It was Huggy Johnson. You might know him.'

'Can't say that I'm familiar with the name,' replied Gribble, still affecting his most nonchalant mien.

'He's bunking down at the livery stable until his daughter arrives on tomorrow morning's stage. Then they're heading for Phoenix to register his claim.'

The agent responded with a lackadaisical nod of the head as if it was of no concern to him. He then proceeded to appraise the item with a magnifying eyepiece. As well as being clued up in assessing gold content, Foxy Gribble was an experienced practitioner in the art of a deadpan portrayal. His guts were churning up. Yet outwardly, a calm and detached manner gave no hint of this fervour.

He carefully studied the said item, turning it this way and that, grunting to himself.

'So what's it worth?' snapped the edgy voice of Kid Streater.

Still the agent hesitated. It was all part of his regular ploy. Finally an assessment was declared.

'Well, gentlemen,' he drawled out. 'This certainly is a reasonable piece of gold you have here.' He paused again, nodding speculatively. The two wranglers were hanging on his every word. 'But nothing special, you understand. I can give you … erm, no more than fifty bucks.'

Streater's eyes widened. That was more than they could make in two months wrangling on a cattle ranch. He looked at his partner. 'What do you reckon, Alamo?'

The assay agent forced his facial expression to remain inscrutable. An apathetic disregard of take-it-or-leave-it indicated that he was doing them a favour.

'Sounds good to me, Mr Gribble,' replied Alamo. 'We'll take it.'

Gribble's whole body relaxed. Yet he still maintained an aloof manner as he counted out the money. 'Glad to do business with you,' he declared, concealing the tremor in his voice with a cough.

He remained still as a statue until the pair of wranglers had departed. Then he leapt into action. The lethargic inertia was instantly cast aside. Locking up the office to prevent any interruption, he hustled into the back room where all his samples and assaying equipment was located. What he sought was a particular ore sample that had been in his possession for over ten years.

The samples were kept in a heavy oak chest bolted to the floor. It was secured by two large locks. The keys were kept on Gribble's person at all times, attached to his watch chain in place of a timepiece.

After opening the chest, scrabbling fingers delved into the heap of gold and silver nuggets, all of varying quality. Each one had a label attached, indicating the ore content and where it had been found. Some were virtually worthless, others of much greater significance. These latter had been acquired from those fortunate jaspers whose pictures now adorned the front office.

The nugget in question was hidden away at the bottom of the chest. This was the first time it had been removed for some considerable time. In the early days following its devious acquisition as payment for a gambling debt, Gribble had frequently laid his avaricious gaze on the unique piece of pay dirt. Its previous owner had claimed it came from the 'Lost Dutchman' mine.

At the time, the significance of this enigmatic hoard had not registered with the gambler. The green baize and pasteboards were his chief means of income. Only later did he learn of the various myths and stories surrounding the famous missing hoard. By then it was too late. The prospector in question had died in a shootout when somebody ambushed him, hoping to learn the truth. Ever since, many intrepid hunters had searched for it. All had failed. And the legend had grown and expanded considerably with the years.

This was the first time any possibility that he might be getting closer to solving the mystery had occurred in Gribble's time as an assay agent. Nervously he picked up the fabled chunk of gold, handling it with careful reverence. A shaking hand fixed the magnifier into his right eye. Sucking in a lungful of air, he brought the new acquisition close. Meticulous study of both fragments required a slow and painstaking approach to ensure there was no mistake in the final analysis.

Once the examination was concluded, the agent needed to sit down. There was no doubt in his mind. The two items were indeed from one and the same source. He removed the eyepiece and once again fastened a bewildered peeper onto the new specimen.

'Have you really come from the Lost Dutchman?' he whispered to himself as if he didn't want to be overheard. 'All this time with nary a murmur, and here you are,' he muttered to the inert chunk, barely able to credit his good fortune, 'sitting here, perky as you please, in the palm of my hand.'

Then his rubicund features clouded over. All he owned

was one nugget. The mine had been re-discovered by this old prospector who was aiming to register the claim in Phoenix. If that happened, Jonas Gribble would be no better off. The devious agent's mind began to formulate some nefarious plot of how he could secure the mine and its vast hidden wealth.

The first task was to identify the miner. Buckskin was full of guys hoping to strike it rich in the rugged mountain country behind the town. How could he pick out one dude amongst that lot? And, more importantly, discover the location of the mine. It could be anywhere within a fifty mile ride. A drink of bourbon helped temper the aggravation seething within the corpulent frame. Then he remembered what those simple-minded cowpokes had said.

The old prospector was called Huggy Johnson and he was meeting his daughter off the morning stage.

THREE

OUT OF THE BLUE ...

Foxy Gribble was up bright and early next morning. It was an unusual experience for the assay agent to witness the golden glow of a new day's sun rising over the Mescals. He was used to a more leisurely wake up call from his landlady at the Frontier boarding house. Breakfast would have to wait.

The twice weekly stage coach from Safford and all stops east could arrive at any time between dawn and midday. It was all dependent on the driver's whim. Some travelled overnight across the Coronado Flats. Others preferred to stay at one of the numerous relay stations.

Klondyke Jessop was a guy who liked to rest up overnight. He was due for retiring in six months. The days of racing across the rough terrain under a silvery moonscape were now a distant memory. He liked his sleep and a good hearty meal at the end of a long day sitting on a hard bench seat atop the bouncing Concord. So this particular arrival did not make its scheduled appearance in Buckskin until noon.

Gribble was more tetchy than a grizzly on heat when a team of six finally staggered to a dusty halt outside the Butterfield depot. Luckily, his office was only one block north so he had a good view of those alighting.

There were only two arrivals. The first was a little guy carrying a large valise, clearly a salesman who hurried across the street to the National Hotel. A young woman followed him.

She paused on the boardwalk, peering around as if looking for someone. She was clad in jeans and a tight-fitting shirt with a plainsman hat perched on her head at a jaunty angle. The red bandanna tied around the swan-like neck assuaged the rustic impression. Gribble's lascivious gaze couldn't help noticing that her trim figure bulged in all the right places. This dame was certainly no cowgirl.

Before he had a chance to further study the newcomer, an old guy stumped out of the depot and greeted the girl with a fond embrace. Gribble's eyes gleamed. This had to be Huggy Johnson, the jasper who had discovered the Lost Dutchman. He wasted no more time. Leaving the office, he strode down towards the couple, affecting an offhand attitude. He leaned against the wall then casually lit up a cheroot.

'It sure is good to see you, Freda,' Johnson espoused warmly, taking charge of her valise. 'Did you have a good journey—'

The girl ignored the query. 'What's this all about, Pa?

Your letter implied it was urgent that we meet up here,' she interjected, setting her hat straight. 'But it didn't give any details. It's lucky that my assistant in the shop was able to take over so I could come down here.'

'How is business in Santa Fe?' Johnson enquired, taking her by the arm. 'You've been running that dress-making shop for two years now.'

The girl brushed off the enquiry with a briskly charged, 'All right, I guess.' She was more interested in her wayward father's earnest summons. Again she pressed home her enquiry. 'What's all the fuss about? It has to be something special for you to bring me all the way down here at such short notice. Your letter did stress the need to come immediately.'

She looked around at the cluster of sun-scorched buildings. The chary regard did not exactly exhibit a wildly upbeat enthusiasm for the town. Buckskin was certainly no Santa Fe with its booming and prosperous trade links to Mexico.

She was tired after the four day journey. A hot tub and change of clothes were needed. But the urgency of the missive had intrigued Freda's sharp mind. She wanted to learn what Huggy Johnson had discovered. It had to be something about his obsession with mining.

They stood on the sidewalk. The nearby presence of Jonas Gribble was ignored as Huggy briefly explained. The Fox stiffened. He was all ears. Maintaining a blasé indifference was almost unbearable. His boots shifted, eager to move closer. The rest of the disclosure was missed. But the sly eavesdropper had heard enough. A covetous glint did not bode well for the innocent young woman and her father.

The pair did not linger outside the stage depot. Already, the old timer was ushering his daughter across the street where he had already booked her a room.

'I've discovered a mine that looks to be one of the richest sources of gold ever found in the territory, maybe in the whole country.' Johnson's voice shook with emotion as he removed a map from his frayed jacket and showed it to the girl. A trembling finger pointed out the position of the finding. 'It's here in the Superstition Mountains. This map will enable the authorities to identify my claim and draw up an official deed of ownership. I need you as a witness when I register it in Phoenix. There's no way I could trust anybody else with a discovery this valuable.'

The old dude's fervent animation was compelling. Freda had grown up with her father's compulsive desire to strike it rich. The family had travelled widely from one boom town to the next. The Comstock Lode, Cripple Creek, Silverton and many others. The most recent was the Vulture Mine up north at Wickenburg. That had been two years before. The ups and downs of prospecting had been exciting in those early days.

But life on the fringe of civilization was tough. Always being on the move from one hit to the next had not suited Martha Johnson. The final straw came following a second failed attempt to hit the jackpot in Cripple Creek. The exasperated wife had run off with a perfume salesman when Freda was only seven.

Huggy had done his best to raise the youngster on his own. But the rough mining camps were no place for children. He laboured long and hard, managing to put enough aside to send her back east to a private school for young ladies. They met up periodically. And it was one of Huggy's more successful ventures that had set Freda up in her own business. For that she would be eternally grateful.

Since then he had stumbled from one meagre venture to another, the proceeds getting fewer as he got older. Regular correspondence kept the girl informed of his whereabouts. But this was the most passionate letter so far.

'I reckon …' He gulped. A lump in his throat made the old dude pause to draw breath before he could continue. '… it could be the fabled Lost Dutchman.'

The blurted declaration brought Freda to a halt halfway across the street, causing a wagon load of pit props to come rumbling to an ungainly halt. Her big hazel eyes widened. Even she had heard of the legendary stash. During her time living in the mining camps, frequent conversations had made reference to the lost mine. Many had tried to locate it, so far without success. Could her own father have stumbled upon the discovery of a lifetime?

'Shift yer ass, yuh stupid old goat,' railed the teamster, bringing them both down to earth. 'Er, not you, miss,' the guy apologized, red-faced, tipping his hat. The duo quickly got out of the way and hurried across to the far side.

Even before they reached the boardwalk, Jonas Gribble was scurrying off in the opposite direction. He needed to have words with a business associate who owned the Rim Rock Saloon. Spider Bremen was a gambler by trade. And not a particularly honest one. Although he was astute enough to keep his hands clean in Buckskin.

Others employed for their pasteboard deviance were given a free hand, Bremen taking a cut of the proceeds. But should their tinhorn manipulations be exposed, he was swift and decisive in dealing out frontier justice. As such, his duplicity in other areas remained hidden, the reputation for running a clean operation unbesmirched.

That didn't prevent him employing a couple of hard-nosed villains. Squint Haikon and Idaho Pete Weller were ostensibly security guards to ensure fair play at the tables and deal with troublemakers. The hired gunnies were slouching on the bar when Gribble appeared in the doorway of the saloon. The place was busy.

All the tables were occupied. Miners sat hunched over their cards side by side with hunters and cowpokes. The house gambler was unmistakeable. Clad in a flashy check suit with velvet lapels, the yellow silk vest was bright enough to hurt the eyes. Not to mention distracting the punters.

In addition to poker, faro and monte were on offer with a roulette table to one side. Raucous calls and shouts punctured the thick, smoke-laden atmosphere as men urged on the clicking dice bouncing around the craps table.

Gambling in the West was a widespread fixation with men betting on anything and everything. Outside the confines of organized gambling, snail races, grasshopper jumping contests and even spitting competitions were all pursued to excess in the hope of earning a few extra bucks. One of the most engrossing spectator sports was cock fighting where hundreds of dollars could change hands.

Most avid participants of the gambling fraternity were cowboys. A pack of dog-eared playing cards was a resident feature in all bunkhouses. No excuse was required for the pack to emerge and a game to be set in motion. Many ranch owners forbade gambling on their premises, especially during cattle drives. Trouble between hands was the last thing they needed.

It was a different proposition when the paid-off hands hit town at the end of a drive. Unfortunately they were no match for the slimy tinhorns whose grasping paws easily clawed the hard-earned dough from their pockets.

Streater was no different. Unlike his partner, the Kid was an avid gambler. Poker was his favoured choice. But all the tables were occupied. Todd Heffridge on the other hand was more taken with the songstress warbling on the stage at the rear of the saloon. The gal had all eyes focussed on her dulcet tones, not to mention the revealing outfit that afforded little to the imagination.

Engrossed in their own activities, it was little wonder,

therefore, that neither of the two wranglers noticed the arrival of the assay agent.

'What should I go for, buddy?' Streater could not make up his mind. 'The roulette wheel or the craps table?' He nudged his partner.

'Ugh?' Alamo was not bothered. His gaze was elsewhere. 'You decide. Don't make no odds to me.'

Bremen was at that moment talking to a saloon girl called Galloping Jane over by the bar. A brash hussy, Jane was renowned for offering a free night of unbridled passion to any guy who could beat her in a horse race. She rarely lost. The poor dupes were then charged double for their effrontery.

She was miffed at not having been given a single day off in the last month. Before the dispute became over-heated, the saloon owner noticed his associate signalling from the doorway. Judging by Gribble's animated gesticulations it appeared to be no ordinary conference that was being requested. He quickly brought the spat to an end by agreeing to Jane's demand for one day off each week.

'But I'll be docking your wages,' Bremen rapped. His bushy eyebrows met in the middle of his forehead. The intimidating trait was used to purposeful effect when browbeating those who challenged his authority. Galloping Jane grunted having little option but to accept if she wanted to keep her job.

The calico queen was immediately forgotten as Bremen nodded for his associate to join him in the office on the upper floor of the saloon.

Once established in the plush privacy of his personal domain, Bremen was quick to question this sudden meeting.

'What's gotten you into such a sweat?' He didn't like being interrupted while dealing with recalcitrant employees. 'It better be good.'

'Take a look at this,' Gribble shot back. He thrust the nugget into the saloon owner's hand. 'And tell me that ain't the finest chunk of paydirt you ever did see.'

Bremen studied it closely. He was no expert when it came to assessing the worth of such items. But that didn't stop him affecting an erudite persona. 'Sure looks a good piece. But what's so darned special about this particular one?'

Gribble lowered his voice, peering around nervously, even though the door was locked and they were alone. 'It's from the legendary Lost Dutchman Mine.' That disclosure certainly piqued the gambler's interest. 'Two dumb clucks brought it in yesterday.' The assay agent produced his own sample to compare it with that recently bought from the wranglers.

Bremen studied it closely.

'They're from the same lode,' Gribble assured the gambler.

'You didn't tell them, did you?' was Bremen's burning demand.

'What do you take me for?' scoffed Gribble. 'I ain't no tenderfoot. 'Course I didn't. But I've just found out who has actually discovered the mine. It's an old dude and his

33

daughter. And they have a map.' He went on to outline the events he had recently witnessed out on the street. 'This is our big chance to snatch the biggest hoard of high grade ever discovered. We'll be the richest guys this side of the Mississippi. Think of it. No more dealing with fractious saloon gals and tinhorn gamblers. It's the high life for us, partner. We can split the proceeds right down the middle, fifty-fifty. So what do you say?'

Bremen was equally smitten by the thought of a life on Easy Street. The two men had undertaken numerous shady deals in the past. Some involved claim jumping, others land acquisition. Gribble had access to information while Bremen provided the muscle. So far the devious partnership had worked well. But this was by far the most profitable venture up until now. The chance to clean up and finally quit this dust-caked hole in the desert.

'I reckon the old guy and his daughter will set out for Phoenix to register the claim straight away,' Gribble hurried on. 'They won't want to waste any time.' His devious mind was figuring out all the angles as he spoke. 'Send Squint and Idaho Pete to ambush them as they go through Tonto Canyon. They should have no problems knocking off an old crank and his daughter. Once the map is our hands, we'll be in the clear. The two of us will have been here in town when the ambush took place. So nobody will suspect a thing.'

'Sounds good to me,' agreed Bremen, rubbing his hands. 'You keep an eye on the old dude,' he said, ushering Gribble over to the door. 'Tell the boys to come up here for their orders.'

Nobody paid any heed to Haikon and Weller sidling up the stairs to the office. All except for Galloping Jane, who was nursing a grudge against her boss. She was still less than satisfied at her treatment by the gambler. A day off with less pay felt like an insult to the important service she provided. So what did he want with those two layabouts?

Everyone else in the Rim Rock had eyes and ears only for Trixie Fontana, known as 'The Little Song Thrush'. Alamo was among them. His partner was still debating which game to play. The lyrical songstress was just a grating distraction to a far more important decision. He shrugged, muttering to himself, 'Guess I'll have to toss for it.' He hooked out a silver dollar and flipped it into the air. Heads for roulette, tails for craps!

But at the precise moment his hand lifted to catch the coin, Alamo nudged his arm with an appreciative comment. 'Ain't this little song thrush some'n else, old buddy?'

The Kid was knocked off balance along with the coin which landed somewhere with a brisk chink. Certainly not in the Kid's hand.

'You clumsy mutt,' Streater complained. 'Now I've done lost my stake.'

More grumbling followed as he dropped onto his knees, searching the dirt-smeared floor. His clawing hands were soon coated in the filth of what felt and smelt like decades of unsightly ordure. There was everything down here including spit and vomit. But a silver dollar could not be ignored. So where in tarnation was it?

Then a call came from above where the croupier was announcing the latest winners of the roulette spin. Still grovelling on the floor, the tetchy wrangler found himself being addressed by the shade-sporting wheel operator.

'This your dollar piece, mister?' The guy bent down, jabbing a finger into Streater's neck. 'It's the only winner this time round and has come up as an eleven-to-one winning streak. That's three horizontal numbers in a line. Your'n were 25, 26 and 27.'

That soon found the Kid stumbling to his feet. 'You mean I've won?' He was utterly amazed.

'That's what I just said, ain't it?' rasped the surly croupier. Any winners in the Rim Rock were not exactly treated like visiting dignitaries. 'That's eleven bucks plus your stake money.' He pushed the winnings across the green cloth.

Streater's mouth opened but nothing came out. He looked like a fish caught on a line. Then it hit him like a loco mule. 'I've won! I've won! Hey, Alamo, for the first time in my life I've beaten the odds at roulette. Ain't this our lucky day?'

Even Todd Heffridge couldn't ignore such a spirited holler. He was equally stunned at this unexpected upward swing in their fortunes. First the gold nugget, now a winning bet in a saloon.

'What you gonna do with it?' he posited.

'What do you think?' Without any hesitation he put

the whole stake of twelve dollars onto number twenty six. 'It can't fail. Not today. Streater's my name. And 26 has to be our lucky number. I can feel it in my bones. That's your age, ain't it?' Alamo nodded absently. The Kid then fished out the rest of his cut from the nugget and added that to the pile on the selected number.

'Don't be such a jackass,' warned his partner. 'Quit while you're ahead. The chances of you winning a second time round are zero.'

But Streater was adamant. He even tried persuading his partner to stake his own dough. 'Come on, buddy. What have you got to lose? A few measly bucks. We still have the chance to work old Huggy's claim if'n things don't turn out. But I can guarantee they will. It's written in the stars.'

'Final bets, please, gentlemen,' the croupier called out as he prepared to spin the wheel. 'You up for this, fella? Or is it too much for you?' The sneeringly offensive tone and derisive look he laid on Alamo Heffridge, as if to say the down-at-heel drifter hadn't the guts to chance his arm, sealed their fate.

Holding the odious toad's gaze, the strong-willed young wrangler added his own poke to the pot. 'OK, mister,' he snapped. 'Spin the wheel.'

By this time, most of the saloon had abandoned their drooling over Trixie Fontana and moved across to view the action around the roulette table. Even the piano player had brought the performance to an untimely halt as he joined the packed throng. The poor gal was left twiddling her tassels. All eyes were focussed on the little white ball as the croupier sent it spinning around the edge of the wheel.

His regular call brought time to a standstill in the Rim Rock. 'Watch the white, there she goes. But where she'll land, no one knows.'

At that moment nothing else mattered except the gyrating turntable and its petite companion. Round and round it went, mesmeric and as alluring as the sway of a rattlesnake's head. Only when the ball ceased its rotation and tumbled onto the numbered divisions could a collective intake of breath be heard.

The ball bounced once, twice then settled on number ...

FOUR

... AND INTO THE RED!

Twenty Six. Silence descended over the gathering. Men stared, unable to believe their eyes. But there it was. The ball was indeed resting in the 26 slot. Even the croupier was struck dumb, flabbergasted. A huge cheer went up. Such a win was exceedingly rare. Raucous congratulations poured from myriad throats.

Ever the scrupulous professional, Jordan Trump the croupier, called for order as he announced the winning sum of money. And it came to over $750. That was more than most of them had ever seen before. Some lucky prospectors had struck it rich in the gold fields. But those fortunate few were not clients of the Rim Rock anymore. They now frequented the more up-market Shady Lady. Only the losers and those who had frittered away their fortunes remained.

The two lucky punters waited to receive their winnings. But they were to be disappointed.

'Sorry, gents,' the now fawning Trump apologized. 'We don't carry that much at the tables. I'll have to give you a promissory note.'

The faces of the two winners dropped accordingly. This was not what they had expected, nor welcomed.

'You ain't trying to cheat us, are you, tinhorn?' growled Streater, bunching his fists.

'Of course not,' protested the croupier. 'The Rim Rock always pays its dues.'

'So when can we claim the dough?' rapped Alamo, who had quickly recovered from the shock of being a winner for once in his life. His tone was terse and threatening.

Trump was sweating and those two security men were nowhere to be seen. Where in thunder had the critters gone when they were needed the most?

'You will have to see the boss about that,' he burbled, handing over the IOU.

'And where can we find this boss?' snarled an equally curt Todd Heffridge.

'He'll be in the office up those stairs.'

Without another word being spoken, the two wranglers turned in the direction indicated. The crowd parted to let them through. Mutterings and comments followed them. This momentous event would be discussed and retold well into the foreseeable future. But all Alamo and his pal were concerned with was their payoff as they stumped across to the stairs.

Kid Streater now received his third surprise of the day.

'I hope you won't forget to buy a gal a drink with your

winnings, Kid.' The expectation was from Galloping Jane.

Streater turned towards the lyrical request, eyes bulging. He would recognize that husky drawl anywhere.

'Madam Channing!' he exclaimed. 'More commonly known as Galloping Jane!' He raised his battered Stetson and made a sweeping bow. The woman responded with a neat curtsey. The bronc peeler went on to satisfy the puzzled look coating his partner's face with an explanation of the odd nickname and how they had met. 'What in blue blazes are you doing down here? Last time we met up was in … Erm, now let me think.' His leathery face creased up in thought.

'Farmington on the San Juan in New Mexico. You can't have forgotten the Golden Goose,' the lady in question declared, jogging his memory. 'I was running the second storey entertainment.'

Streater threw his buddy a knowing wink. That was one period in his colourful life deeply imprinted on his mind.

'Only joshing,' he responded with a lusty chuckle. 'Boy, do I just. And you sure gave good service. I ain't got no complaints in that department. So how long you been down here?'

'About six months now,' Jane replied. A doleful expression clouded the ageing madam's painted façade. 'But it ain't the best move I ever made.'

'How d'you mean?'

'Spider Bremen, the boss, is a right skinflint. Tight as a banker's fist. Reckon I'm gonna pull out if'n things don't improve.' The woman lowered her voice, realizing that walls have ears. Not to mention nosey bartenders. 'Word has it that he's into a heap of shady deals. Just watch your step, boys.'

That was when Alamo butted in. 'Hey, Kid! Ain't you gonna introduce me to your friend?'

'Oh yeah, I clean forgot,' Streater apologized. 'This is my partner, Alamo Todd Heffridge. We're just on our way upstairs to see this skinflint saloon jasper. The two of us have won a hefty wedge on the roulette table.'

'So I saw. Spider ain't gonna be too pleased about that,' the woman cautioned. 'You watch him. That scheming rat is craftier than a weasel on the prod.' The sour grimace was transformed into a dazzling smile as she turned to Alamo. 'Pleased to meet you, Todd.' They shook hands. 'Perhaps I'll see you boys later when you've coaxed your winnings out of that sly dog.'

'You can bet on it, ma'am,' said Alamo, tipping his hat.

They then mounted the broad flight of stairs, turning right at the top into a corridor. Spider Bremen's office was at the end. His name was emblazoned in gilt lettering on a fancy sign. Without bothering to knock, they burst in on the startled saloon owner who was at that moment studying some papers behind his large desk.

He lurched to his feet, clearly angered by the unwarranted interruption. The thin slash of a mouth gave the hard-nosed businessman a permanent sneer.

'What's the meaning of barging in here unannounced? This is a private office. Only employees are allowed in. And they knock first.'

'This here promissory note needs honouring,' rapped Alamo, ignoring the protest as he slapped the said paper down on the desk. 'And we want paying off right away.'

When Bremen looked at the note, his eyes widened. 'I don't carry that amount in the safe,' he quickly declared. 'You'll have to wait until I visit the bank. Buckskin don't have one. The nearest is in Phoenix.'

'And how long will that be, mister?' a narked Kid Streater butted in. 'We ain't got time to hang around here. You best pay up or else.' His hand slid down to the old cap and ball Navy Colt on his hip.

'Now take it easy, boys,' Bremen said, raising his hands. An oily smile attempted to placate the two wranglers. 'Don't worry. You'll get your money. Honest Spider Bremen, that's what they call me. And I always honour my debts. Now, seeing as you're both keen gamblers, how's about we toss for it – double or quits?' He pulled a silver dollar from his pocket ready to flip. Dupes like these two were always ready to chance their arms. 'Fifty-fifty. Two-to-one odds. That's fair, ain't it?' But a crafty glint in the trickster's eye did not auger well for the result.

'If'n you can't cough up our winnings,' Alamo snapped, cutting off his partner's acceptance of the bet, 'how d'you figure to pay us double?'

Then he lunged at the gambler. Bremen was caught out by the sudden move as Alamo snatched the coin from his hand. Turning it over, a hard twist of the lip saw him grabbing the saloon boss by the shirt front. Buttons popped, followed by a harsh tearing of the ruffed cotton.

43

'You dirty chiseller!' he snarled. 'A double headed coin. Just as I thought. House wins every time.' The Army Remington appeared in his hand. 'I ought to fill you with lead right now. But that won't get us our dough.'

'You reckon he's holding out on us, pard?' Streater added, ready to join the affray. 'Ja...' In the nick of time he realized that mentioning the source of his information by name could have dire consequences for the saloon madam. 'I hear tell this guy can't be trusted with a stick of candy.'

'We'll soon see. Lock the door, Kid, so we won't be disturbed.' The gun prodded the gambler's exposed chest. 'Now you open the safe, mister, and let's find out what you're hiding in there.'

Slowly the gambler placed a key in the lock and opened the heavy steel door. He bent down with his back to the two punters and reached inside. But his searching hand ignored the piles of dollar bills. Instead he felt around for the small Hopkins and Allen .32 pistol he always kept inside the safe for just such an emergency as this.

'OK, you win,' Bremen apologized, evincing a contrite and forlorn bleat. 'Guess I should have known you guys were sharp cookies. Here's your money.' He turned to face the two men, the gun firmly held. It swung ready to spit flame and death.

In the nick of time, Alamo saw the danger. He roughly pushed his buddy to one side. The small gun exploded. For such a small weapon it produced a deafening roar in the confined space. White smoke poured from the barrel.

The slug buzzed the Kid, missing his head by a whisker.

Alamo replied with two bullets from his own pistol before the tricky gambler could get off a second shot. A cry burst from Bremen's mouth as he fell back, clutching at his hand. The pistol lay on the floor blasted to bits. But the harsh rattle of gunfire had not passed unnoticed. Already, somebody was hammering on the door.

'You all right, boss?' It was the panic-laden voice of Jordan Trump. More thumping followed. All hell was breaking loose on the far side of the door. It would not take long for them to break it down. Then the fat would really be in the fire.

'Come on, pard,' Alamo hollered out. 'We need to get out of here.' He turned for the rear door which led out into a back alley.

'Not before we claim our dues,' Streater declared, hunching over the open safe.

'Just take what we're owed,' shot back the young wrangler. 'And hurry up about it. That door lock is ready to bust wide open.'

Streater merely grabbed a handful of bills without bothering to count them. 'This'll have to do,' he said, following his partner out the back way.

'You thieving rats won't get away with this,' the injured gambler shouted. Already he was struggling to his feet.

Luckily for him, Alamo's shot had only grazed his hand. He paused in the exit and pumped a couple of shells at the shaking office door. They were deliberately aimed high to prevent injury. The last thing the two wranglers needed was a murder charge hanging round their necks. Shouts of alarm indicated that the brittle warning was effective. The door ceased its tremulous quivering. It afforded them breathing space even if the reprieve was only temporary.

Their horses were still tethered outside the office of the assay agent. Hurrying along behind the row of buildings, the two fugitives emerged gingerly onto the main thoroughfare two blocks down. All eyes were fixed on the Rim Rock saloon. Nobody noticed a pair of stealthy wranglers quietly mounting up and spurring off down a side entry.

'Phew, that was close,' Streater wheezed once they had cleared the outskirts of Buckskin. 'But at least we got our dough.' His breath was pumping out in short gasps. 'Guess I'm getting a mite old for this sort of excitement. Maybe we can persuade Huggy Johnson to take us on as partners in the mining claim he's registering now that we're in funds.'

'First we need to get clear of Buckskin,' Alamo cautioned, peering over his shoulder to ensure they were not being followed. 'Those guys ain't gonna be too pleased with a pair of wranglers dishing their lowdown scam.'

After receiving their orders from the boss, Squint Haikon and his sidekick had made surreptitious enquiries about the old miner and his daughter. The ostler down at the livery barn told them that the pair had left Buckskin soon after dawn, driving their wagon. That meant they had a good six hours start on the two bushwhackers.

'If'n they're driving an old beat-up crate, the main road to Phoenix by way of Domino Sink is the obvious route,' commented Pete Weller. 'We could take the old Indian trail over Pinal Pass and cut them off.'

Haikon nodded his agreement. A shifty smirk creased the gunman's warped face.

'They can't get up much speed in a wagon. So that should give us time to catch them in Tonto Canyon.'

'Why do you figure the boss is so eager to get rid of the old timer and his daughter?' asked the mystified Idaho gunslinger.

'He wants a money belt the old dude is toting,' replied Haikon. 'Reckons there's a map inside showing the location of a gold mine.'

'It must be a valuable one if'n the boss is going to all this trouble,' Pete eagerly commented. 'That means we should be in for a hefty bonus if'n this pays off.'

The two hard cases spurred off along the main highway out of Buckskin. After two miles a narrow trail branched left along a draw. It soon began to climb steadily into the foothills of the Mescal Range. This way was rougher but much more direct compared to the main Buckskin-Phoenix route.

After a couple of hours, the two bushwhackers were through the notched gap of Pinal Pass and descending the far side. They had pushed their mounts hard all the way to reach the ambush site at Tonto Canyon ahead of their quarry. Yet still they were too late. The dust cloud ahead informed them that the wagon had reached the canyon ahead of them.

Peter Weller cursed aloud. 'The darned critters have beaten us to it. What we gonna do, Squint? There's no chance of overtaking them now in this gorge.'

The accepted brains of the unholy partnership, Haikon glared at the yellow twirl of dust. His lazy eye twitched irritably. The result of a knife fight over a dame in the Cagebird Dancehall in Tucson, the injury had left him with a permanent lopsided balance to his skeletal features.

That single flick of a blade tip had transformed the handsome visage into something resembling a gargoyle. An unsightly alteration that had turned the regular cowhand into a brutal killer. The only crack of a smile that split the misshapen visage these days was when Haikon was using his beloved Colt revolver.

While the two gunmen were grumbling, Huggy Johnson had spotted them.

'I don't like the look of those two behind us,' he growled, slapping the leathers to urge the two horses up to more than walking pace.

'You reckon they could be after the map, Pa?' his daughter replied nervously.

'Somebody in Buckskin could have overheard me talking about the mine and figured to snatch it afore we reach Phoenix.' The old miner cracked his whip, spurring the horses to greater speed. But they were freight hauling nags and unused to moving above a slow trot. The pursuers were drawing ever closer.

'It could be those two wranglers you told me about,'

Freda concluded, glancing behind. But at this distance and with the rising dust devils obscuring her vision, it was impossible to put names to faces.

'Whoever it is, they ain't gonna have my map,' snarled the miner, although he had now come to realize that their wagon could not outrun any saddle horses. 'At the next bend in the trail, I'll hop off and keep these jaspers busy while you ride on ahead. There ought to be a trading post coming up soon where you can get help.'

'I don't want to leave you, Pa,' the girl objected. 'It don't seem right. And I can handle a gun as good as any man.'

But Johnson was adamant. 'Don't argue, girl. This ain't the time or place to worry about what's right. Just do it.'

He dragged on the reins, hauling the team to an ungainly halt. Leaping off the wagon, he grabbed a hold of the ancient Springfield breech loader and a handful of cartridges. Freda hesitated. But her father vigorously waved her off. Then he settled behind a rock to await the pursuers.

Minutes later the two suspicious travellers were met with a loud blast from the rifle. The .45 calibre rifle bullet lifted the hat from Weller's head.

'That was a warning shot. Don't come any closer,' bawled the irate miner. 'Next time it'll be for real.'

Both men skidded to a halt and quickly sought cover. Gunfire was exchanged. But Huggy had chosen a good position. He was well placed to keep the two men pinned down. In addition to the Springfield, he also had a .31

Manhattan five shot pistol. But he was limited by the small number of cartridges he had for the rifle.

By contrast, the two bushwhackers had the latest Colt .45s and Winchester carbines. But they did not want to hang around. Unlike the miner, Squint Haikon was well aware that some four miles up the road was the Burnt Oak Ranch. Their missed opportunity to ambush the miner in Tonto Canyon had brought them rather too close for comfort. The gunfire might be heard, encouraging an unwelcome investigation as to its cause.

'We need to get this over with fast,' he hissed to his partner. 'You circle around behind the critter while I keep him busy.'

Weller nodded as he crawled off behind some boulders. Five minutes later, a signal told Haikon that his buddy was in position. Levering and firing the repeater with accomplished precision, he had no difficulty in keeping Johnson's head down. That enabled Weller to emerge from cover and sneak up on their quarry unobserved.

Haikon made certain the miner's attention was focused on the front as he called out,

'You can't get away, old man. Better to surrender the map now and save yourself a heap of grief.'

'I'd rather die first than submit to dry-gulching skunks like you.' To emphasize his obstinate stance, another shell from the rifle clipped the rock behind which Haikon was concealed.

'Looks like your wish is going to be granted, mister,' the squinter replied.

'What you talking about, scumbag?"

'Just take a look over to your right and you'll find out.'

'You can't catch me out with that old trick, fella,' Johnson guffawed.

'It's no trick, buster.' The gravel-tainted voice had indeed come from Johnson's blind side. Pete Weller stood there, legs akimbo, a revolver poised for action.

The miner swung to face the unexpected danger. But it was too late. The six gun bucked twice. Both slugs found their mark in Huggy Johnson's weathered torso. He slumped over, gasping out his final seconds, cursing his naïvety.

Weller strolled across, blowing the smoke from his pistol barrel. The gunman's face cracked in a vicious smile. 'Guess you were a mite foolish to figure on bucking the odds.' Not the slightest hint of remorse softened the killer's craggy face as he pumped a final slug into the soft tissue. Johnson was dead before his head slammed into the hard ground.

The two assailants wasted no time. A quick search of the miner's body revealed the all-important money belt strapped round his waist.

'This is what we're after,' Haikon rapped out, unfastening the heavy belt. He then frisked the miner's pockets. 'And it feels like there's some dough in here.'

'Finders keepers, don't you reckon, buddy?' Weller declared. 'Nobody's gonna know about this wedge of dough. All the boss wants is the map.'

'We'll split the money on our way back to town,'

concurred Haikon, quickly taking charge of the unexpected bonus. He stuffed the greenbacks into his pocket then looked around. Nothing moved amidst the sterile landscape. Unless you counted a small herd of mule deer crossing the trail up ahead. But that didn't mean the gunfire had passed unnoticed. A nervous reaction caused his lazy eye to flicker. 'Now let's get out of here. This guy's daughter must have taken the wagon on ahead. Help could arrive at any moment.'

And help did indeed arrive. But from a different source than they expected.

FIVE

FALSE ACCUSATION

Alamo Todd and the Kid had also been hoping to catch up with the miner. But their intention was of a more practical nature. They were intending to take Johnson up on his offer of work. They were also hopeful that the money they had won on the roulette table might buy them a part share in the proceeds of his mining venture. But that all depended on them getting clear of any pursuit by the cheating Bremen.

The sound of gunfire was something that took them by surprise.

Rounding a bend in the narrow gorge of Tonto Canyon, they were just in time to spot the two bushwhackers robbing the body of a man lying on the ground. A couple of shots soon drove them off.

'You reckon that could be old Huggy down there?' asked a shocked Kid Streater. 'Although there's no sign of the girl or the wagon.'

'Whoever it is sure needs our help,' said Alamo.

'We're getting to be a right pair of goodwill Charlies,' Streater muttered, spurring off after his buddy.

The bushwhackers had a good start. But their pursuers were keeping pace. One of the outlaws turned and fired. At that distance, he had no chance of scoring a hit. Nevertheless, it informed the shadows that these guys meant business and had no intention of meekly surrendering.

At the exit from the canyon, the terrain opened out. That was where Haikon and Weller split up, one heading east, the other west. The pursuers were stymied by this unexpected manoeuvre. They dragged their sweating mounts to a halt, unsure how to proceed. That delay was enough to enable the killers to make good their escape. Alamo railed at the disappearing clouds of dust. Venting their frustration, the two men replied with shots of their own.

'All we can do now is go back and see to the poor jigger they've robbed,' he fumed impotently. 'Let's hope our intervention was in time.'

They swung around and rode off back to the site of the ambush. It was indeed Huggy Johnson. But he was beyond help. Both men hung their heads. All they could do was stand there looking down at the blood-stained corpse.

That was when a bunch of riders appeared round the up-trail bend in the canyon. In the lead was a lean-limbed guy whose hard grey eyes bore into the two wranglers. More important for Alamo and his buddy was the shiny tin star glinting on the sheriff's vest. Clay Bowman was accompanied by a group of six other equally dour-faced deputies. They quickly surrounded the two suspects. All had guns that were pointing at the two wranglers. They must be a posse returning to Buckskin.

The gruff voice left them in no doubt as to the lawman's judgment of the grim setting. Two men standing over a dead body clutching smoking revolvers. Could it be any clearer? And the sharp challenge that followed brought the obvious assumption to its blunt finale.

'Drop those hog legs and step away from the body, you murdering pair of scum.'

The order needed no explanation, the intimation was crystal clear. Any resistance would see them joining poor Huggy in the hereafter.

That was the moment Freda Johnson arrived. She leapt off her wagon. A cry of anguish issued from her distraught features as she cradled the inert body in her arms. Tears poured down her pale cheeks. It was a heart-rending sight to see the girl rocking back and forth in torment.

'It was lucky for Miss Johnson that we were heading back this way when she met up with us on the trail.' The sheriff's gun hammer clicked to full cock. 'If'n you can call it luck, seeing as how you two skunks have just murdered her pa.' A rancid growl had crept into the lawman's command. 'Now do as I say and shuck them guns pronto, else there's gonna be a triple burial.'

Alamo and his buddy quickly obeyed. But they were not slow in protesting their innocence. 'It ain't what you think, Sheriff,' Alamo insisted, stepping forward.

But he was struggling to comprehend what was happening. Suddenly their whole lives had been turned upside down. Out of the blue, they'd played the good samaritan, receiving a valuable gold nugget for their assistance. Now they'd been plunged into the red, falsely accused of murder. It was mind-numbing. And this grim-faced tin star was unbending.

Yet still a protestation of innocence had to be attempted. 'We heard shooting and came here hoping to save this guy. Unfortunately we were too late. The killers fled when they saw us.'

'So we chased after the rats,' butted in Streater, 'but they—'

'Yeah, I know. They separated, giving you pair of humbugs the slip,' interjected the angry starpacker. It was a bald statement of fact rather than a question, and chock full of blunt-edged sarcasm.

'How did you know that, Sheriff?' enquired a bemused Kid Streater.

The lawman punched out a mirthless guffaw. 'You thick-headed saps. Don't you think I ain't heard that weak-kneed excuse before? You two are guilty as sin. It's written across your ugly faces, clear as daylight.'

'OK, Hank,' the lawdog called to his chief deputy. 'Shackle these two critters good and tight. They're coming back with us to Buckskin ... and a necktie party.'

Blood drained from the faces of the two captives. Sheriff Bowman's cold utterance had brought home the dire circumstances into which they had blundered.

'Now raise your hands and stand still while I search you.' The sheriff roughly frisked the prisoners but found no incriminating evidence.

It was Hank Wardle who made the critical discovery. 'Well, look what I've found,' he hawked, gleefully lifting the wedge of greenbacks from Alamo's saddle bag. The find only added to their grim prospects.

It was immediately assumed this was what the killers were after. Freda had not mentioned anything about the map or a money belt. All she was concerned with at the time they met up was saving her father from the robbers.

Bowman waved the money in front of the two men. 'So this was what you were after.' He spat in the dust. 'A man's life snuffed out by a pair of robbing sidewinders.'

Streater was dumbfounded. It was left for Alamo to proclaim their innocence with vigour even though it fell on deaf ears. 'We won that money fair and square on the roulette wheel.'

The plea was ignored. The posse had their killers. Clay Bowman was a solid lawman not inclined to look elsewhere for answers. In his eyes the case was clear cut. Who else could have shot Huggy Johnson? And now they had a motive – robbery. These jiggers must have followed the miner out of town and took their chance when the opportunity arose. What they hadn't bargained on was a posse being close by. Otherwise they would have escaped free as birds.

The watching posse grumbled and growled. Some of

them were already reaching for lariats. Why wait until they reached town? In the Arizona of the 1870s, frontier justice could be harsh and unyielding. Only a stoic regard for upholding the law by Sheriff Clay Bowman kept them in check. He was not called Rockwall for nothing. Bowman quickly picked up on the men's anger.

'There'll be no vigilante justice while I'm wearing this,' he rapped, jabbing the legendary badge of office. 'You guys got my drift?' Probing eyes black as thunder challenged the posse to buck his authority. None did. 'OK, Hank, you heard what I said. Now shackle up those prisoners.'

'Sure thing, Sheriff,' replied the deputy. 'Give me a hand, Lucky.' As if a dish of water had been poured over a fire, the threat of vigilante action had been effectively quashed. Such was the esteem in which Rockwall Clay Bowman was held.

Freda Johnson was unaware of the latent friction, so consumed was she with her grief. But now, that angst was quickly transforming into a mist-shrouded fury at the perpetrators of the heinous crime. She lurched to her feet, throwing herself at the nearest of the two alleged killers.

Small fists pummelled the broad chest of Alamo Heffridge. Any attempt to ward off the blows was prevented by the shackles holding his arms behind his back. Still, he made little attempt to avoid the beating. The girl had every right to be so distraught even if it was towards the wrong culprits.

Only when a fist drew blood from a cut cheek did Sheriff Bowman reluctantly intervene, drawing her away.

'Don't worry, miss,' he assured her. 'I'll see to it that these two receive the full weight of Arizona justice in a court of law.' Then he turned back to his chief deputy, Hank Wardle. 'You and a couple of the boys load the body into Miss Johnson's wagon. Then we'll head back to Buckskin.'

After making a successful escape from their pursuers, Haikon and Weller met up a half hour later at Pinal Pass.

'That was good thinking,' Idaho Pete remarked to his partner. 'Splitting up sure foxed those jaspers. Any ideas who they were?'

'Just an unlucky chance meeting.' Haikon shrugged. 'Don't matter none. We threw them off the scent, that's the main thing. Now let's get back to town pronto. And not a word about that dough. What the boss don't know won't hurt him.'

They arrived back in Buckskin by the same route they had taken on their outward journey. It was quicker, but more importantly, would avoid any meetings that might later be recalled. Robbery and murder were not to be taken lightly, especially with a law dog of Rockwall Bowman's measure running the show. They entered the town through a jumble of back lots and shacks. Nobody saw them tie up outside the rear of the Rim Rock saloon. A quick look around and they hurried up the back stairs.

Bremen had been on tenterhooks ever since his two

cohorts had left on their precarious mission. Each knock on the office door had found him edgy and terse.

'Who's there?' he snapped.

'It's us, boss, Squint and Idaho,' came back the muted reply. 'We snatched the goods you wanted.'

Bremen leapt to his feet and shot over to the door. He peered outside to ensure his bodyguards had not been observed. This was a matter that needed keeping under wraps.

'Anybody see you coming up here?'

'We came in the back way, boss,' replied Haikon. 'Nobody spotted us.'

The men entered at a nod from Bremen. 'Let's have it then,' he ordered. Haikon handed over the money belt. Feverishly, Bremen extracted the all-important map. He opened it up, a wicked smile cracking the tight façade. 'This is gonna make us all rich, boys. Did you have any trouble nabbing it?'

The two outlaws had agreed to tell it as it happened, omitting their retention of the dough in the belt. There were also some small samples of ore which Bremen was examining with interest.

'These must be the samples from the mine the old dude was hoping to register in Phoenix. I'm gonna do it in his place.' His face clouded over as their account of the gruesome incident reached its conclusion. 'Did those two interfering drifters see your faces?'

'Not a chance, boss,' scoffed Weller. 'They were too far away.'

'Good,' grated the saloon owner. 'And not a word about this to anyone, understand? This is between the three of us.' Bremen's fixed stare emphasized the need for prudence.

'What about Gribble?' Haikon asked. 'He's gonna want his cut.'

A sneaky grin boded ill for the assay agent. Bremen paused, handing out cigars. He didn't respond until they were lit. 'You leave Jonas Gribble to me. That sucker ain't gonna be too pleased with what I have to tell him.'

The two minders gave the sly comment a quizzical frown. But they did not pursue the matter. They were only the hired muscle. Spider Bremen had the brains and the natty duds that accompanied his successful connivance. He turned towards the iron safe and carefully locked the money belt containing the all-important map inside it.

'You boys have done well,' Bremen praised his men, handing them fifty bucks apiece. 'You can also have one of these nuggets each as a bonus. There'll be a lot more coming your way when I've lodged that claim to the Lost Dutchman. Go have yourselves a good time downstairs while I wait here to deal with Gribble. I'm sure he'll be coming over here soon.'

Sometime later, the expected knock came on the back door. Bremen was ready. His call for the visitor to enter failed to conceal an edgy rasp. It was indeed Jonas Gribble. And the assay agent came straight to the point.

'Did you get the map?'

The sly gambler's woebegone expression did not bode

BAD DEAL IN BUCKSKIN

well. Bremen shrugged his shoulders. 'My boys lost him. The critter must have taken a different trail to outfox any skulduggery. And he darned well succeeded.'

Gribble eyed his partner-in-crime with a dubious expression of scepticism. He was not convinced. 'You ain't holding out on me, are you, Spider? We're supposed to be partners in this venture. Fifty-fifty right down the line. That's what we agreed.'

'I'm as unhappy with what's happened as you.' Bremen accentuated his own frustration at the supposed failure to secure the vital document. The classic gambler's deadpan regard was compelling and persuasive. 'All I can do now is send the boys out again to try and cut him off before he reaches Phoenix. But I ain't holding out much hope. Like as not he'll already have registered his claim.'

Bremen laid an arm across the agent's shoulders, offering commiseration as he walked him to the door. The sooner he was rid of this turkey the better. 'There'll be other chances to make our fortunes. Just keep your eyes and ears open. And remember that I'm always ready to back your play.'

The gambler's credible blarney allayed the agent's suspicion. He was still downcast when he left the saloon. But at least he knew that the Lost Dutchman was no figment of the imagination. It was somewhere in the vicinity. But that was no real consolation knowing that it was now out of his reach. All he could hope for was that some other mugs would give him the opportunity to make a fast buck. By using the back stairs behind the saloon and the other premises, Gribble did not witness the arrival of Sheriff Bowman and the posse. Their two dejected prisoners were hustled into the jailhouse and locked up.

Freda Johnson carried on down the street to deliver her father's corpse to the undertaker, receiving the assurance that he would let her know when the funeral was to take place. On the ride back to Buckskin, she had made up her mind to head back to Santa Fe. There was nothing left for her here now. Grief is a terrible affliction. But at least the killers were now locked up. It had made her determined to erase the whole sorry business from her mind.

She retired to her room in the National Hotel to be alone with her loss. After crying herself to sleep, the girl awakened some time later in a more calculating frame of mind. Her thoughts went over the grim events of the previous day. And after due consideration, a much more measured assessment of the robbery and its aftermath prevailed. And her attitude noticeably hardened.

Those killers had stolen the money belt containing the map. But according to the sheriff, it was not in their possession when he had searched them.

So where could it be? They must have buried it somewhere in the vicinity of the killing ground, hoping to return at some future time. But the arrival of the posse had scotched their nefarious scheme.

After mulling over all her options, Freda finally decided to stick around. She could take over her father's cabin in the foothills of the Mescals. It would provide a fitting base from which to conduct a search of the area before registering the claim under her own name.

But first she had to find out if her theory regarding the missing money belt would bear fruit, or more to the point, the vital map. Without that, she could not continue her father's dream of registering the Lost Dutchman in her own name. Unlike Spider Bremen and the duplicitous assay agent, greed was not her motive. Freda felt she owed it to her father's memory. The old guy had laboured half his life trying to locate the fabled hoard. And then, at his moment of triumph, those dogs had cut him down.

The thought made her both angry and distraught in equal measure.

Once she was settled in the cabin, then she would return to Tonto Canyon. The only problem was, she had no idea where the cabin was located. She was mulling over this problem when a knock came on the door.

'Who is it?' the girl called out, reaching for the Manhattan pistol she had taken from her father's body. The grim experience had made her fully aware that the cliché of the Wild West was no idle invention of dime novelists. It was only too real. The gun was now pointed at the door.

'It's me, Sheriff Bowman, miss,' the gruff voice announced. 'I was just wondering if'n you needed any help while you are in Buckskin.'

She was about to thank the man for his offer but decline when the notion struck her that this man might know where her father had lived for the last couple of years. Without any further hesitation she called out for him to enter. Once in the room clutching his hat like a tenderfoot suitor, Freda posed her query.

'I intend taking up residence there and carrying on from where he left off. That is providing I can locate this mine he wanted to register.'

Bowman sucked in his cheeks. He was a guy from the old school who believed that a woman's place was in the home doing domestic chores. What this girl had in mind was man's work. 'This is mighty rough country, ma'am,' he cautioned with a shake of the head. 'Not the place for a woman to be living alone.'

Freda's lithe frame stiffened, the look arrowed at the lawman noticeably hardening. 'I can take care of myself,' she shot at him. 'And that's not what I asked you.'

She stuck her chin out assertively, cowing the tough lawdog who was taken aback by this woman's feisty manner. Then she waited, large eyes locking onto the weathered face. Bowman needed time to gather his wits together. More at home dealing with hard-nosed villains, this woman was way outside his experience. Like a lion tricked by a tiny mouse, the formidable town-tamer felt that he was the one who had been tamed.

'S-sure, I know where old Huggy had his place,' was the somewhat chastened reply. 'I've passed through that way a number of times in the course of my duties. If'n you are still intent on going out there, I'd be happy to escort you.'

Freda's face softened, her belligerent stance easing

back. 'That sure is a thoughtful gesture, sheriff. And I'd be pleased to accept. How are you fixed for this morning? I would like to get started as soon as possible.'

Although Clay Bowman had a dozen or more tasks that should have taken priority, he immediately tossed them aside. 'I'll be ready to ride within the hour if'n that's all right with you, Miss Johnson?'

'Call me Freda ... Clay, isn't it?'

Red-faced and bashful, hard-boiled Rockwall Clay Bowman was like the cat that got the cream.

SIX

A TASTY SURPRISE ...

Meanwhile, Alamo and Streater were languishing in a grubby cell inside the jailhouse. Two days had passed. With nothing to do except count the adobe bricks, time hung heavy. The circuit judge was not due to hold court in Buckskin for at least another month. Boredom and impotent frustration were being overshadowed by the threat of the hangman's rope.

'How can we prove our innocence when the real killers got clean away?' grumbled Streater, lying on his bunk. 'Nobody is gonna believe us.'

'We have to find some way to get out of here,' Alamo railed, slamming a bunched fist against the bars of the cell door. 'These jaspers are gonna string us up for sure after the trial. They don't have any other suspects. It'll be an open and shut case.'

'Less noise in there,' shouted Deputy Wardle, who was wading through a pile of wanted dodgers in case these two were among them. Although elected officers of the law were only entitled to a partial cut of any reward money, that could add up to a sizeable chunk of dough. 'Otherwise I'll gag you both and forget about supper.'

Supper! That was a joke. Alamo muttered the disparaging opinion under his breath. All they'd had so far were some tepid leftovers that the pigs had refused. And the coffee tasted like dishwater.

Kid Streater in particular was suffering. The older guy sure enjoyed his grub. Alamo could usually get by on anything. It came as something of a surprise, therefore, when Galloping Jane Channing walked through the door. And clutched in her hands was a sandwich cake coated with chocolate icing and cream in the middle.

'That for me, Jane?' asked Wardle. His mouth was watering as bulging eyeballs latched onto the tasty treat.

'All in good time, Hank.' The saloon gal winked. 'This one is for the prisoners. I felt sorry for them stuck in here on prison rations. So I baked a cake special.'

Wardle was instantly suspicious as to why this dame should be bothered about two killers. 'What's so special about these varmints?' he posed sceptically.

'We know each other from when I worked up north,' she replied with nonchalant ease, having expected the distrustful young deputy to question her motive. 'They treated me well and paid up on time for services rendered. I can't believe they murdered someone in cold blood.'

'We caught them red-handed,' Wardle averred. 'The skunks were stood over the body still holding their guns.

Ain't no doubt in my mind. They're the killers all right.'

Eager to bring the young deputy round to her view-point, she hurried on. 'There'll be one for you later if'n you'll grant them this one little favour.' Her heavily made-up eyes fluttered provocatively, hinting that more than just cake would be available should he agree to her proposal.

Wardle was a young sprout, cocky and full of his own ability to replace the ageing Rockwall Bowman at the next election. He also had a potent appetite for the more earthy pleasures on offer in Buckskin.

The latest visitor to the jailhouse was well aware of his libidinous proclivities which included frequent visits to the top floor of the Rim Rock where Jane held sway. It was that weakness she intended to exploit to the full. Ripe lusciously red lips and a heaving bosom drove the true reason for Jane's magnanimous gesture from the drool-ing Wardle's mind.

As was her avowed intention, the poor sucker was mesmerised, hooked and landed. Any reservations now floated out the window. Lust-filled eyes eagerly devoured the tempting spectacle now swaying provocatively before him. These older queens sure knew their business when it came to boudoir capers.

'G-guess th-that will be all right,' he spluttered. 'J-just slide it under the feed bar at the bottom of the door.'

Jane had purposely waited until Sheriff Bowman was out of the way. She had seen him heading out of town, accompanying the dead miner's daughter. For what she had in mind, the Rockwall would have instantly smelt a rat and curtailed her supposed act of kindness.

Hank Wardle on the other hand was a pushover, an easy target. And she was confident that her forthcoming deception would not be revealed afterwards. It was highly unlikely Wardle would ever admit that a woman had been the cause of what Jane had in mind. Embarrassment and the dread of being taunted thereafter for his gullibility would ensure he devised a suitable excuse to cover the loss of his prisoners.

Sashaying across the room, her potent gaze locked onto that of her old associate. 'You boys enjoy this cake. I made it with my own fair hands.' She paused, offering Streater a meaningful lift of the eyebrows. 'It contains only the finest ingredients. Make sure you eat every last morsel. It'll sure lift your spirits.' Then she pushed the cake inside the cell before turning to leave. 'See you around, fellas.'

To the ogling Hank Wardle she murmured in a tantalizing burr that sent a shiver down the poor guy's back. 'You too, handsome.' The lascivious wink effectively sealed the deputy's fate as she left the office.

'That sure was good of Jane, don't you reckon, buddy?' proclaimed Streater, taking charge of the splendid donation. 'That gal allus did have a heart of gold.'

Unlike his pard, the Kid had not cottoned to Galloping Jane's clandestine stratagem.

'Just like the cake, old buddy,' muttered Alamo in a throaty whisper. 'Just like the cake.' Keeping a weather eye on the still mesmerised deputy, he pulled the Kid to one side where the lounging Wardle could not see them.

Streater instantly caught on to Alamo's stealthy behaviour. 'What's bugging you?' he queried, adding with a curt guffaw, 'It's only a cake. Don't reckon there's a nugget hidden inside it, do you?'

'No, but there could be something much more useful to our current predicament.' Still, the Kid did not catch on. 'Do I have to spell it out? She's put something inside the cake that could get us out of here.'

'You reckon?' blurted out Streater.

'Keep your voice down,' Alamo cautioned, slapping a hand over the Kid's mouth. 'The last thing we need is Wardle cottoning to Jane's wily game.'

Without further ado, he carefully lifted the top layer of sponge. And there it was. A piece of cloth was wrapped around a hard metal object. Kid Streater was now staring hard as his buddy uncovered and removed … a tiny Remington .41 twin-shot Deringer. Both men looked at each other in surprise. For a moment they were bowled over, stunned by this sudden reversal in their fortunes.

It was Streater who broke into the taut silence. 'Well, I'll be a horned toad!' he exclaimed, struggling to contain his elation. 'That gal sure is a diamond, a regular life-saver.'

'I ain't about to argue there,' concurred an equally startled Todd Heffridge. 'All we have to do now is work out how we're gonna play this.'

Streater's initial elation was curbed when the consequences of Jane's magnanimous gesture lodged itself in his brain. His reply was circumspect. 'I'd hate to think that Jane will land herself in hot water for helping us out like this. She's bound to come under suspicion when Bowman comes back to discover we've flown the coup.'

Alamo was more pragmatic. 'She ain't no mooncalf. You saw the way she handled young Wardle. Had him eating out of her hand. She knows that if'n the truth of this ever comes to light, he'll never hear the last of it. But I'll make sure he thinks otherwise.' He tapped his nose before quickly revealing what he had in mind.

A quick peep through the bars of the cell revealed Deputy Wardle toying with a quill pen. It was obvious that his mind was not on the job allocated by the sheriff of checking the store rental accounts. Jane Channing had seen to that. Alamo knew that they had to act fast before that hard-nosed sheriff returned. The problem was drawing the deputy over to the cell where they could see him properly.

Then it came to him, out of the blue. A flash of inspiration. Without consulting Streater, he called out loud enough for the wistful young deputy to hear.

'This cake sure is delicious, ain't it, Kid?' He took a bite of the tasty treat. There was no denying that what he had said was the truth. In addition to a horse racing track, it appeared that Galloping Jane knew her way around a kitchen as well.

'Sure is,' agreed Streater, backing his partner's play. 'Jane always did bake a fine cake. She learnt the art from her mother.'

'You can have some if'n you've a mind, Deputy,' Alamo offered. 'There's more than enough for us all.' The munching and slurping noises were exaggerated to deliberately coax the young guy over to the cell door.

And the ploy worked. Seeing that cake made Hank Wardle feel hungry for inner sustenance as well as that of a more seductive nature. His stomach was rumbling. He stood up and ambled across to the cell. Meanwhile, Alamo had handed the cake to his partner and stepped to one side.

'Just hand him the cake with a smile on your kisser,' he whispered, 'I'll do the rest.' The small gun was hidden in the palm of his hand ready to produce at just the right moment. As soon as Hank Wardle appeared round the corner from where he had been sitting, the Kid moved closer to the bars ostensibly to hand over the alluring comestible. That was when Alamo made his play.

'Stay right where you are, and don't make a move,' the wrangler hissed. 'This little beauty packs a hefty sting when it's riled.'

Wardle was shocked by this sudden turning of the tables. Streater dropped the cake and reached through the bars, snatching the deputy's holstered revolver. Now two guns were covering him.

'Step over to that rack and bring the keys here.' The startled deputy was still too stunned to comply. 'Move your ass, dipstick. Or I'll ship you to the Devil's Kitchen!' The blunt threat brought Wardle back down to earth.

'Where in thunder did you get that gun?' It hadn't yet

registered in his lethargic brain that Jane Channing was the cause of his chagrin. That would come later. Time was now of the essence to ensure they made a clean getaway.

'The keys, lamebrain. We ain't about to stand trial for a crime we didn't commit.' The two guns persuaded the lawman that discretion was the better part of valour. He moved across to the key rack and brought them the right one. Streater grabbed it and unlocked the cell door. The hapless deputy was then bundled inside and locked in.

That was when the nickel dropped. 'It was the cake, wasn't it? Jane hid that peashooter in the cake.'

Alamo shook his head as he buckled on his gun belt. 'You should have taken our boots before tossing us in the slammer,' he declared, edging the deputy away from any condemnation of Jane Channing. 'But I suggest you eat the rest of that cake to get rid of the evidence before Rockwall Bowman comes back. That guy ain't gonna believe for one second it was merely an innocent gesture of kindness on Jane's part. You getting my drift, mister? Best you start figuring out a more suitable reason for our sudden departure.'

Hank Wardle slumped down onto the bunk inside the locked cell. The reality of what he had allowed to happen was indeed surging to the forefront of his thoughts. Alamo decided to nudge his brain in the right direction. 'Just remember where that Deringer was hidden. Saves you having to answer a lot of awkward questions.'

The idea of a loophole excuse had been well and truly planted. Now it was time to scarper. Luckily their horses were still outside.

A quick scan of the street in either direction revealed nobody close by. Most importantly, Clay Bowman was not around. Trying desperately not to rush, they sauntered across to the hitching rail and mounted up.

'We'll go down the side alley beside the jail to avoid being spotted,' Alamo affirmed. 'That way, nobody will know which direction we've taken.'

Once clear of Buckskin, they headed up into the line of ponderosa pine trees behind the town. Only when they were ensconced within the comforting verdure was the young wrangler able to relax. Winding up through the densely packed ranks, they finally emerged onto a plateau. No words had been spoken in the gloom of the forest. Once out in the open, Streater quickly took heed of his partner's pensive glower.

'Some'n bothering you, Alamo?' he asked. 'You ain't said a word about where we go from here. Any ideas sprouting in that devious mind?'

Deep lines of thought ribbed his buddy's forehead. 'I've been struggling to figure out how those jaspers knew about old Huggy's map.'

'Could be it was just a random heist,' suggested Streater. 'A couple of jaspers on the prod who got lucky. And we nearly messed up their plan.'

'Too much of a coincidence for my liking, them being in Tonto Canyon at just that moment.' Alamo scratched his head. 'I reckon it was set up, a pre-arranged ambush.'

'Who would have worked that out?' objected Streater.

'We are the only dudes who knew about the map, except Huggy and his daughter.'

They rode on in silence, each man trying to work through the conundrum. And all the time they were heading in the direction of the ambush site. Alamo hoped that the Tonto Canyon would provide the answer.

He voiced the idea that had formed in his head. 'If'n those guys were only after money, they would have discarded the money belt. But we never saw it, did we?' Streater shook his head in agreement. 'That means it could be somewhere in the vicinity. Let's go take a look around. We might even find the map.'

They both spurred off, eager to reach Tonto Canyon and hopefully solve the dilemma and clear their names. Having a robbery and murder charge hanging over their heads was not to be taken lightly. Already a posse could have been despatched to hunt them down. That likelihood was enough to see the two innocent fugitives constantly panning the landscape for any signs of pursuit.

A circuitous route finally brought them to the macabre site of the crime. By avoiding the main trails, they had thankfully encountered no other humans. Caution dictated a measured approach to the Canyon entrance. Briefly, Alamo paused at the spot where the two killers had split up.

He dismounted and poked around but there was nothing suspicious to be seen. If anything was to be uncovered, it stood to reason it would be close to the killing ground. They pushed on into the enclosed confines of the Tonto. Knowing what had happened here sent shivers down the spines of both riders. It was the chilling awareness that they were the chief, indeed the only suspects.

'This is it,' Alamo croaked. His throat was dry as the desert sand as he looked down on the dark stain. It took some effort to shake off the macabre reaction. 'Let's see what we can find.'

They split up and began searching through the undergrowth of cat's claw and saltbush scattered amidst the boulder-strewn enclave. It was a daunting task. For the next hour the two partners meticulously scoured the rock-strewn basin of Tonto Canyon. The blistering heat had turned the enclosed confines of the ravine into a cauldron. Sweat poured off their faces. Streaks of high cloud, white lines starkly etched against the deep azure stood little chance in countering the pitiless sun.

The killers had not been accorded much time to hide their stash, if indeed there was anything to find. Yet the longer Alamo hunted around, the more he was forced to the unwelcome conclusion that no obvious clue as to their identity, nor indeed their haul, would be forthcoming.

Streater was sitting on a rock taking a breather on the far side of the canyon. A languid hand wiped the sweat from his grizzled features. Alamo had decided to join him and reluctantly proposed they abandon the search. He turned away from the cluster of boulders he had been searching when the silence was broken by the deep-throated roar of a rifle.

SEVEN

... AND AN UNEXPECTED TWIST

Alamo whirled round, his hand reaching for the holstered revolver.

'Hold it right there, mister.' The cutting directive was incisive. 'One false move and you're buzzard bait. Now slowly turn around. And get them mitts in the air.'

Caught off guard by the sudden termination of their search, Alamo slowly obeyed the speaker. The short-lived chance of freedom so abruptly curtailed was a stunning blow difficult to accept. Not least because the speaker was of female origin. Legs akimbo and confidently in charge, Freda Johnson stood there clutching the Henry carbine she had taken from Alamo's saddle. And she clearly knew how to use it.

Even more surprising was a headless rattlesnake not two feet away on a rocky ledge. Even in death it was still thrashing about. So intent had the searcher been in his quest that the basic rules of survival in wild terrain had been tossed aside.

'That critter was about to lunge,' the girl announced, keeping the gun aimed at Alamo's chest. 'I could have let the serpent have his way. But that would be doing the hangman out of a job. And in any case, there's a question that needs answering before you bite the dust.'

'I'm beholden to you anyway, Miss Johnson,' declared the helpless captive. 'Those varmints always did give me the creeps.'

The girl ignored the thanks. More important matters needed explaining. 'How did you manage to escape from jail? And what are you doing out here?'

'That's two questions.' Alamo's perky remark was joined by a smile. Relief was etched across his face, knowing that the girl was alone and not part of a posse. But his growing confidence and attempt to defuse the tense situation fell on deaf ears.

Freda Johnson was not about to capitulate to the charms of the rampant lothario – Alamo Todd Heffridge.

'Don't try being funny with me, mister,' she growled. Her back stiffened, lending emphasis to her inflexible stance. 'You shot my pa in cold blood. I aim to make you pay the ultimate price for that. Now answer the damn questions, you lowdown rat! My trigger finger is getting mighty itchy.'

The girl's blunt demand was punched out with more venom than the dead rattler. She meant business, and was holding the hardware to back it up. Far from cowing the young wrangler as intended, her blunt manner only served to enhance her allure in his wandering eyes. She sure was feisty, but no less attractive for that.

Unfortunately, in Freda's zeal to neutralize the alleged killer, she had overlooked the fact that he had a partner.

Kid Streater now made his presence felt. Emerging from behind a clump of teddy bear cholla, the Kid crept silently up behind the oblivious girl. Alamo's face remained impassive as he tried to hold Freda's attention so as not to give the game away.

'I had a little help in getting out of the slammer.' He chose not to elaborate, hurrying on. 'Then I came looking for some clue that might prove I had nothing to do with your father's shooting.' The conscious insinuation was that he was alone. All the same, his avowed assertion was not play-acting. 'You have to believe me. I had nothing to do with it.'

'Why should I?'

But she was given no further opportunity to express her disdain. The Kid's hand shot out and grabbed the rifle. Before the girl realized what was happening, she had been disarmed. A cry of fear mingled with anger at being caught out escaped from her open mouth. But she quickly recovered, launching herself at the object of her aversion. Alamo easily held her off.

'Quieten down, can't you?' he urged, firmly pushing her away. 'What I've said is the truth. And I'll prove it.' Then, much to her surprise, he took the Henry from his partner and offered it back. 'Here, take it!' The resolution was solid. 'If'n you're convinced we're guilty, then pull the trigger now and get it over with. Nobody will blame you for defending yourself against a couple of ruthless killers.' Freda took a hold of the rifle and swung it towards them. Both men stood their ground, waiting for her to pull the trigger. 'If'n that's what you think, then do it!'

In truth, Alamo sensed that this girl had no intention of carrying out the grim execution. It was not in her nature, nor that of any right-minded woman. Nevertheless, it was still a hairy moment as her conscience silently fought a battle with the Devil's malevolent tongue inside her head. And there was no denying that she was still good and mad. Anything could happen when someone was that angry.

The tense moment dissolved as quickly as it had blown up. Still clutching the gun, she sank to her knees. Her head dropped. Tears flowed down her silken cheeks. It was left to this handsome stranger to extend the consoling hand of support. Briefly she allowed him to hold her shaking body. Then she shrugged him off, still not convinced.

'If it wasn't you who shot Pa, then who did? I came out here hoping to find the stolen money belt. When I saw you here, what was I expected to think?'

Given the opportunity to proclaim their innocence, Alamo wasted no time in firmly presenting a solid case in their defence. Freda allowed him to explain all that had happened during the last few days. From their meeting up with Huggy Johnson to the jailbreak assisted by Galloping Jane Channing. This final declaration brought the first smile to Freda's aquiline features since her father's brutal shooting.

'That guy deserves to be taken down a peg or two,' she declared acidly. 'Even before I'd delivered Pa's body to the undertaker, he was pestering me.'

But the thought of Hank Wardle being bested by a cake made her laugh out loud. The unexpected softening of Freda's attitude saw her whole face light up. From a pretty girl she had been instantly transformed into the most beauteous creature Todd Heffridge had ever laid his appreciative gaze upon. The girl was totally unaware of the effect she had interposed on the young wrangler.

'Perhaps I did jump the gun accusing you guys like that. You can't blame me.' To consolidate her acceptance of their innocence, she laid the carbine aside. 'But there still remains the main problem of who actually did kill my pa.'

'I've been giving that some thought as well,' Alamo agreed. Relief at having brought the girl round to their position eased the tension in his tight muscles. 'And I've only just realized that only one other person knew that nugget came from the Lost Dutchman.' He paused to let the import of his forthcoming indictment sink in. 'And that was Jonas Gribble, the assay agent.'

Freda jumped in to add grist to the mill. 'Did he have greasy black hair parted down the middle and a moustache like a fat slug taking refuge under his nose?'

Both men howled with laughter. 'Gee, ma'am, don't that beat all,' exclaimed Streater, slapping his thighs. 'A fat slug! I couldn't have put it better myself.' He twirled his fingers suggestively. 'All black and hairy to boot.'

'Ugh!' The colourful description produced a grimace of revulsion before Freda continued. 'Well, he was lurking near the Butterfield stage depot when I arrived from Santa Fe. Never gave it any thought at the time. I just figured he was a loafer passing the time of day. The sneaky toad must have heard everything that passed between Pa and me. And more to the point, he must have spotted the map.'

'It's obvious that Gribble must have been behind the ambush then,' snapped Alamo. 'The skunk hired a couple of gunslingers to rob poor Huggy and steal the map.'

'What can we do about it now?' asked Streater.

'We have to find Gribble and get him on his own.' It was clear that his pard was intimating a return to Buckskin. 'Then we can force him to tell the truth. That's the only way we're gonna clear our names.'

Streater was not so eager. And he expressed his contradictory view in no uncertain manner. 'You crazy, boy? That'll be like putting our heads in the lion's mouth. I'd rather stay free with a price on my head. There's bound to be a posse out looking for us. And that deputy ain't gonna be too particular about bringing us in alive when he catches up with us. Not after we showed him up like that. He'll want revenge.'

But Alamo was living up to his stubborn disposition. 'Well, I for one don't want to be on the dodge for a crime I didn't commit. Waiting around for some trigger-happy bounty hunter to drill me in the back is no life for anyone, especially when you're innocent.' His harsh tone soon modulated. He had no wish to fall out with his old pal. 'We gotta go back, Kid. Don't you see? And at least try to put things right.' Then he perked up as another thought struck him. 'Sure there'll be a posse out after us. But they'll figure we've made a run for it. The last thing to cross their minds is that we've stuck around.'

Freda agreed with the insistent Todd Heffridge. She patted the uptight bronc peeler on the arm. 'Alamo's right, Kid. And I can send them on a wild goose chase when they call at the cabin to check up on me. That should give you some breathing space to discover what really happened here in Tonto Canyon.'

'It makes sense, Kid.'

With the two new allies working in unison, Streater was quickly brought round to his partner's viewpoint. The young wrangler's concern now switched to Freda Johnson's welcome change of mind.

'I don't want to be the cause of placing you in any danger,' he stressed. 'These guys are ruthless. They'll go to any lengths to achieve their evil ends. The killing of your pa proves that. Too many people have bit the dust looking for the Lost Dutchman over the years. I sure wouldn't want you to join them.'

Todd Heffridge's sympathetic concern for her well-being was touching. It further helped to soften the girl's attitude towards the wronged man and his buddy. But her fiercely independent character now elbowed to the fore.

'I can look after myself,' she asserted with vigour.

'Those skunks are going to pay for what they've done. And I want to be there at the finish.'

The fiery stance, highlighted by a pink tongue that slid seductively along her upper lip mesmerised the poor guy. It was Streater who nudged his partner back into the realms of the here and now. 'She's made up her mind, boy. Best we get moving.'

So it was agreed. Alamo and Streater would head back to Buckskin while Freda returned to the cabin in the Mescals. Their parting was a somewhat stilted affair. Both displayed the coy bashfulness of two young people on the cusp of a new beginning, though neither was sure how it would end.

It was Freda who broke the knotty impasse by planting a brief kiss on his cheek. Nothing too incendiary, it nonetheless brought a flush of delight to Alamo's tanned features.

'You come and visit once this business is over, y'hear? Look out for War Bonnet Rock. I'm easy to find from there.'

His yearning gaze followed her passage as she rode off. One last swivel in the saddle and a quick wave of the hand before she disappeared from view effectively sealed the young guy's fate.

'You sure got it bad this time, buddy,' commented the perceptive Kid Streater.

There was no response from Alamo. A dewy-eyed gaze was still fixed on that bend in the trail. Was she the one that guys talked about? Love was a word that had never previously been a part of his vocabulary. He had known plenty of women. But none matched up to Freda Johnson. And it had nothing to do with the fact that she might well become the richest gal in the West.

EIGHT

SKIN DEEP

Their return to Buckskin followed the same outward trail. A meeting with the posse led by the indomitable Rockwall Bowman did not bear contemplating. Few words were spoken. Hank Wardle would also be avidly seeking to avenge his humiliation at their hands. Each man was cocooned inside his own pensive reflections.

As they neared the town, Kid Streater's thoughts shifted to a fervent hope that Galloping Jane had not suffered by helping them escape. He had always held a candle for her. They had even once talked of settling down together. Lack of funds and the Kid's itchy feet had failed to make it a realistic proposition. And so the pair had drifted apart. But he was older now. The fancy of such a gal taming his restless spirit was more appealing.

It was soon after the final break that Streater had teamed up with Todd Heffridge. Both men had found themselves working for an outfit that busted wild broncs for the army up in Colorado. They each harboured a great respect for their equine associates. Streater had perfected a method of taming the animal's naturally ebullient spirit without compromising its ability to carry out human commands. It was infinitely more humane than the regular harshly applied busting technique.

But it demanded more time. And therein lay the bugbear. Some bosses were supportive of the Kid's technique. But most just wanted a fast turnaround to make more dough. On this occasion the Kid found himself on the receiving end of more than a tongue lashing when he went against the ranch owner's brutal approach.

Alamo had just returned with a fresh batch of wild mustangs from the high country. Even before he entered the holding corral, he eyeballed the head honcho Arby Snatch laying into the pinioned Streater with a bull whip.

The two had spoken little during the weeks they had been working for Snatch. But that didn't stop the younger guy from butting in. He was well aware of the little jasper's ideas for taming horses and supported his methods.

So far, however, the need to earn good money had won the day. It appeared that Streater had had enough of Arby Snatch's high-handed manner and taken steps to oppose him. He was now paying the penalty.

Alamo ran across the corral, knocking aside the two bulky critters who had spread-eagled the Kid over a wagon wheel. Three blows fell on the poor guy's bare back before Alamo could grab the whip from Snatch's hand.

'What in hell's teeth are you doing, boy?' ranted the

irate boss. 'Get them mustangs into the corral pronto. This has nothing to do with you.'

'It does when you're beating on my buddy,' replied the incensed young peeler.

Snatch wasted no time in fruitless arguments. 'Grab him, boys,' he ordered the other two men. 'This meddling toe rag can join his partner on the other wheel.' He then called across to some men who had just emerged from the bunkhouse to investigate the commotion outside. 'Over here, you guys. I need help to remind these troublemakers who's running this outfit.'

The paymaster had spoken. Both Todd Heffridge and the Kid were popular bronc peelers. But money talks. The three men hustled across the open yard.

Alamo knew that he had to act fast to avoid joining his new buddy at the end of the twitching serpent. The nearest dude who had been holding Streater made to grapple Alamo to the ground. The younger man easily evaded the clumsy manoeuvre, planting a straight left to the guy's jaw. He swayed back on his heels, colliding with his associate. Both men tumbled over the prone form of Kid Streater.

The boss had stepped back. 'A week's pay for the man who brings this skunk down,' he shouted, certain that the bonus would work its magic.

A gun appeared in Alamo's hand. Two shots over the heads of the three approaching wranglers effectively stifled their eagerness to tackle the miscreants.

'Stay where you are, fellas,' Alamo cautioned them. His voice was measured, the warning coolly delivered. 'I'd hate to take any of you down. Our beef ain't with you. But I will if'n the need arises.' The composed yet chilling manner, and a rock-steady gun hand ensured that no amount of dough was worth a plot in the graveyard. They had all seen the accuracy of Todd Heffridge's shooting ability in a recent contest in the nearby town of Dolores.

Streater was quickly helped to his feet. Backing off across the corral, they mounted up. The cocked revolver ensured that no move was made to stop them.

'Ain't none of you yeller bellies got the guts to tackle this turkey?' Snatch bellowed angrily. A shot from Todd's revolver lifted his hat. Another spun it away like a flying plate. That tricky manoeuvre soon shut the guy up. There was nothing like the threat of lead poisoning to quench a braggart's pomposity.

'Don't try following us,' came the blunt directive as the empty Remington was holstered. 'This Henry is fully loaded.'

In minutes they were out of pistol range and heading south towards the sprawling rough country of the Mancos Plateau.

That had been three years before. And they were still together, dodging bullets and angry bosses. A team, a partnership, each looking out for the other. It had stood them in good stead so far. And Alamo was confident their corresponding talents would outwit any huckster who tried pulling the wool over their eyes.

Jonas Gribble had a lot to explain away. And his responses had better be the right ones. The young wrangler's stony regard did not augur well should the devious parasite try to play him false.

'I sure hope you know what you're doing, Todd.' Streater was still not fully convinced they were doing the right thing. The two pals were sitting astride their horses inside the tree cover overlooking the town in the basin below. Vindictive eyes were fixed on the assay office. At this time of day, the slippery dick ought to be in there. Unless he'd already taken steps to search out the secret mine.

'All we can do is head down there and hope that he's still around,' Alamo replied. He nudged his mount down towards the town, keeping a watchful eye open for any hint that they had been spotted.

The man in question was indeed in his office. And his face was purple with anger. He was carefully studying some small nuggets recently offered to him by Bremen's two gorillas. The hard cases claimed they had won them in a poker game from a miner. Gribble had no reason to doubt their story. He paid over the cash value in good faith.

Only later when he studied them closer did the truth dawn. That was when he realized they hailed from the Lost Dutchman. Again he assiduously studied every facet under the magnifier. It was true. There was no doubt in his mind. That two-faced bastard Spider Bremen had double-crossed him. Those two varmints must have waylaid the miner and stolen the map. And now it was in Bremen's possession.

Unfortunately for Bremen, he had made the grave

error of trusting his men's judgement. Hard cases like Haikon and Weller took orders and carried them out to the letter. But the acumen to think for themselves was distinctly lacking. It never entered their sluggish brains that Gribble would recognize the stones.

'So you're figuring on cutting Jonas Gribble out of the picture, are you?' the resentful trickster growled, thumping the counter in rage. 'Nobody does that and gets away with it,' he railed to himself, unaware that he was being covertly watched from the dirty window overlooking the rear of the premises.

'Looks like we're in luck,' Streater whispered. 'And he's alone.'

'You keep a lookout in the front office while I persuade the rat where his best interests lie,' Alamo growled. 'And I ain't gonna be too subtle with my methods.'

As luck would have it the door was unlocked. Gribble had only secured the front, not expecting any disturbance from the rear. He was to be sadly disappointed. Quick as a flash, Alamo was through the door. Streater wasted no time in pushing on to keep watch through the front window.

'You and me have some issues to sort out,' Alamo declared softly. 'You can make it easy or tough. Don't make no difference to me. But one way or another, I intend getting the answers I want.'

Gribble quickly recovered from the unexpected shock of being confronted by the guys he'd duped. He adopted a quizzical frown of ignorance. 'I don't know what you're talking about.'

'I figure you do,' was the snappy reply as the young wrangler lit up a cigarillo.

The supercilious sniff from Gribble did not help the guy's case. Alamo took a step forward. 'I reckon you know exactly what I'm after.' His mood had noticeably hardened. The measured approach was shunted aside, replaced by a much tougher stance. 'The map, asshole. The one you stole from Huggy Johnson after gunning him down in cold blood. Now hand it over. I'm taking it back to his daughter. But not before I hand you over to the sheriff.'

But the agent was still not overawed. He had bested too many naïve punters in the past. Guys who had initially tried threats and intimidation efficiently neutralized. Guile and cunning were Jonas Gribble's stock in trade rather than brute force. Words were his ammunition.

Yet what this guy had just said turned his guts to jelly. So the old miner was dead, in addition to his map having been stolen? And this turkey thought Jonas Gribble was the killer. Their accusation merely confirmed his own suspicion that Bremen had betrayed him. Still he maintained an aloof disdain.

'You can't come barging in here dictating the odds to me,' he snapped back. 'I'm a respected citizen in this town. Who's going to believe a couple of escaped jail birds? The death of that old dude had nothing to do with me.'

Alamo sensed that the time for violent measures had arrived. His manner changed abruptly. 'This is your final warning. Now cough up or else.'

A bunched right fist curled back, ready to do the business. Yet still the assay agent prevaricated. 'You have this all wrong, mister,' he countered in an attempt to sew doubt in their minds. 'It wasn't me that robbed the old timer. I haven't left town for over two weeks. Ask anyone, they'll tell you.'

In that he was telling the truth. More importantly, Gribble was also now fully cognisant regarding Spider Bremen's skulduggery. The swindling cheat had brazenly claimed his men had failed in their mission. That alone made him mad as hell and in consequence, more inclined to deny any involvement.

Alamo was through talking. He wasted no more effort on verbal persuasion, lunging at the repellent chiseller. Gribble was caught on the hop as a solid right was planted into his guts. A left hook then connected with the prominent jaw, sending the victim sprawling onto the dirt floor. Blood poured from a split lip as the assailant hovered over his victim like a predatory eagle.

'Now talk, damn you! Or you'll get more of the same. I ain't leaving here without that map.'

'But I don't have it,' wailed the frightened man, trying to scramble away. 'You've got the wrong man.'

'If'n it ain't you, then who is it?' Alamo was all set to continue the beating when his buddy called out from the front office.

'The posse is back, Todd. And they look none too pleased.' There was a distinct note of panic in the revelation. 'I reckon we ought to make ourselves scarce.'

94

That announcement enhanced the agent's bravado. 'You two are gonna be in big trouble now,' he crowed, scrambling out of reach. 'I'll see to it that you're both arrested. And this time you won't escape.'

His mouth opened to yell out a warning. But he wasn't allowed to deliver the threatened exposure. Alamo drew his pistol and slammed the barrel across the sneering rat's temple. Gribble went down in a heap, groaning and clutching his sore head. The bleary-eyed confusion prevented any chance of a warning cry being raised.

His two assailants quickly backed out of the premises at the rear. Streater was all for making a hurried exit from the town. But Todd had other ideas.

'We'll stick around and see what Gribble does,' he insisted when his buddy raised the obvious objections. 'The skunk ain't gonna spill the beans on us. He's in this scam up to his grubby neck. If'n there's somebody else involved as he claims, odds are that he'll contact them. And soon. All we have to do is stay hidden and see where he goes.'

'The longer we hang around here, the more chance there is of Bowman spotting us,' protested Streater. 'I don't fancy ending up in that cell again. Next time the only way out will be a one-way trip to the hanging tree.'

'Then we'll have to make certain they don't find us.' Alamo was already scanning their surroundings to find a suitable hideout. 'When somebody is out searching, where is it they rarely look?'

'I ain't got time for riddles, buddy,' stuttered the

decidedly nervous Kid. 'Just tell me what's on your mind, then let's scarper.'

A thumb jabbed up towards the passing clouds. His partner's eyes lifted. 'That's right,' Alamo concurred. 'Most folk never look up. So that's where we'll be.' Not entertaining any further discussion, he scurried across to the flight of steps leading up to the second storey veranda encircling the block of stores. 'Come on!' he rapped, urging Streater to follow. 'We'll have a grandstand view from up there.'

They padded quietly up to the railed veranda. Making certain to keep below the edge, they crawled round to the front. It was true. Five minutes they waited. And in that time nary a soul looked up.

The posse had dispersed by the time Jonas Gribble emerged from the office. It was like Alamo had predicted. The prowling snake had no wish to encounter anybody associated with the law. The furtive manner made it obvious he was up to no good. He looked around to ensure that his recent visitors had skedaddled before hurrying up the street. As expected the upper reaches never received a glance. Two sets of penetrating eyes followed the devious trader.

The only problem was that he soon disappeared from view beneath the overhanging veranda. Alamo cursed. It was a snag he had not foreseen. All they knew was that he had gone to warn a confederate. But who was that mystery partner in crime?

'That's torn it!' exclaimed the disgruntled wrangler.

'How we gonna learn where the critter's gone now?'

'Over there,' hissed an animated Streater, pointing to the far side of the street. 'It's Jane. She must have seen where he went.'

The saloon girl was sashaying along the opposite boardwalk on her way to start her afternoon session at the Rim Rock. Like all the other people around, she had not spotted the two hovering birds up on the veranda. The two flyers quickly hustled back down to ground level.

Streater was about to cross the street to intercept his old flame. But Alamo held him back. 'Not so fast, pard,' he said, indicating the approach of an old adversary who was crossing the street clearly with the intention of intercepting Jane Channing. 'That's Wardle and it looks like he's about to hassle Jane.'

A rumbling growl built up in Streater's throat. It sounded like a mountain lion ready to pounce. And so was the Kid when he witnessed the irate deputy roughly grabbing hold of the woman's arm. Alamo had to forcibly restrain the impulsive action that would surely have signed their demise.

'Take it easy, Kid,' he urged. 'Jane's a tough lady. She can look after herself. Any heavy stuff and he knows that she's gonna reveal his humiliating part in our escape. You charge out there now and we're sunk.'

Streater was breathing hard. The realization that he actually loved the woman had prompted the automatic response to rush to her aid. Did the dangerous situation she had engineered to affect their escape from jail mean that she felt the same? His mind was in a quandary.

But Alamo was right. No sense in burning their bridges. They still held the whip hand. But he remained on tenterhooks watching the heated conversation from their hidden position behind some bales of hay. The woman appeared to have gained the upper hand as she pushed past the deputy and stormed off, leaving him red-faced and disconsolate like a kicked dog.

A broad grin split the Kid's face as he slapped his thigh. 'She sure looks to have given him a flea in his ear,' was his animated reaction.

His pal was already thinking ahead. 'All we have to do now is attract her attention without revealing ourselves.'

Galloping Jane was living up to her name as she hurried across the street. Her unanticipated delay by Hank Wardle had made her late for the start of her shift. And Spider Bremen was a martinet when it came to good time keeping. She had no wish for a dock in her wages.

Streater picked a stone up off the ground. A quick glance around to ensure he was unobserved, then he hurled it to land ahead of the woman's path. The missile bounced some six feet away. That certainly caught her attention. Pausing midway across the street, she aimed a caustic glower towards where the missile had originated. Her immediate assumption was that troublesome kids were to blame.

A look of stunned surprise found her jaw trailing on the ground when she spotted the avid gesticulations of Kid Streater hovering behind some hay bales. He and

Todd Heffridge were the last people she had expected to see back in Buckskin. Yet here they both were, large as life.

Jane shrugged off the startled episode that had frozen her to the spot. A quick look around to ensure Hank Wardle was out of sight, then she casually sidled across to where the two men were lurking. Without uttering a word, she ushered them down a back alley.

'What in the name of Hades are you galoots doing back here?' she demanded, pulling them both out of sight behind a shed. 'Hank Wardle is spouting fire and brimstone at the way he was hoodwinked in the jailhouse.'

Streater could barely contain his elation. 'Boy, that was some stunt you pulled, gal. And all to enable us to escape. Don't know how we can ever repay you.'

'By not getting yourselves caught again, that's how,' admonished the dame frostily. 'So what's brought you back here? I figured you'd both have crossed the border by now and be safely out of harm's way.' She was good and angry. But it was all a sham. Jane was indeed glad to see the two partners again. But equally fearful of the danger to which they had returned. 'This place has been buzzing since the death of that miner. Bowman and his underling are convinced it was you. And they'll do anything to track you down. I know you two fellas had nothing to do with it. Have you any ideas?'

'We sure do, gal—'

But Alamo quickly cut off any explanation. 'It's a long story, Jane,' he interposed. 'And we don't have time for it now.' He went straight to the crux of the matter. 'Did you see where Jonas Gribble went after he left his office just now?'

'So that slimeball is involved, is he?' sneered the woman. 'I might have known. He went straight into the Rim Rock. And he was clutching a blood-stained bandanna to his mouth. That wouldn't have anything to do with you, would it?' The heavily rouged features creased in mocking vilification.

Streater chuckled. 'My buddy here was trying to persuade him to spill the beans. But the posse arrived back afore we could make him talk. So we had to scarper pronto. Looks like that saloon boss could be running the show.'

Todd Heffridge's startled lift of the eyebrows said it all. 'You could be right, Kid.' So Gribble had been telling a dash of the truth after all, albeit a much amended version. 'It sure is looking that way. Makes sense when you think it over. Gribble is no hard-nosed gunslinger. He would need the heavyweight backing of a rat like Spider Bremen to pull off the scam.'

There was only one way to find out if his contention held water. They would have to get closer. And that meant another visit to the saloon boss's private domain on the second floor.

NINE

NOT SAFE ENOUGH

'Now you boys take care,' Jane warned the two buddies. 'These guys play for keeps. I'd hate for anything bad to happen now we've just gotten re-acquainted after all this time.' Big soulful eyes settled on the older man, urging him to heed her advice.

Streater's legs turned to jelly. He gulped, swallowing down the lump in his throat. Even though Jane Channing was well past her prime, the Kid could hardly credit that such a delectable dame would look twice at a no-account like him. She still had what it took. Ample proof of her alluring power even with young sprouts like Hank Wardle had shown itself in the way she induced their jail break.

A sound like a choking bullfrog emerged from the open maw. He finally managed to splutter out a reply. 'Going in there is the only way to prove we had nothing to do with that killing.' This was the first chance they'd had to thank the girl and allay any fears she might have harboured regarding their innocence. 'All we were doing,' the Kid stressed, 'was trying to help a poor guy out when Sheriff Bowman came along.'

'I know, honey,' the woman purred. 'Never figured for one moment you'd have pulled a stunt like that. Just watch your back. And never fear. I'll be waiting when the dust settles.'

The husky drawl washed over the smitten guy like melted chocolate. 'That's all I needed to know.'

A brief touch of hands followed before Alamo cut in on the fomenting intrigue. 'I hate to break this up, folks. But we need to press on. Even now those two rats could be hatching a plot.'

'There's a way into the Rim Rock up the back stairs,' Jane proposed, reasserting her cool poise. 'It leads straight to Bremen's office.'

Alamo nodded. 'We used it the last time we made the skunk's acquaintance. This time he'll get the surprise of his life. Come on, Kid. Let's get moving.'

'Keep that perty head of your'n down, Jane,' a concerned Streater pressed the saloon madam. 'I aim to come back here and make an honest woman of you.'

A smile lit up the calico queen's face. 'I'll be waiting, Kid. Don't disappoint me.'

Tears trickled down her pancaked cheeks, smudging the thick make-up. It was a sight rarely seen. Jane always maintained a tough, no-nonsense persona. It was her stock-in-trade. The Kid felt privileged. A final quixotic look passed between them as Streater followed his pal. All their attention now had to be focussed on the upcoming confrontation.

Guns drawn, they hurried down a passageway two blocks down from the Rim Rock past the back of the Sugarloaf Diner and a meat emporium until the back stairs of the saloon were reached. Nervous eyes flicked about to ensure their movements were not being followed. Apart from Galloping Jane Channing, every man's hand in Buckskin was against them.

That thought alone was enough to precipitate a rash of sweat to break out on Streater's face. He stroked it away. But the fear remained. It would stay until they had cleared this nest of vipers for good.

An ungreased door creaked, otherwise only a couple of prowling alley cats were on the move. One had a mouse between its teeth. A fiendish glare challenged the intruders to snaffle its meal. But the two men had more important matters on their minds.

Pausing at the bottom of the stairway, Alamo said, 'You go get the horses and bring them back here. By then I should have the map and we can skedaddle.'

'You sure you can do this without my help?' grumbled Streater. Fearful he might be, but the stocky rannigan was not lacking in pluck or courage. Come hell or high water, he would back his partner to the hilt. 'These jaspers ain't about to surrender without a fight.'

'I can handle a lowdown chiseller like Bremen,' was the firm reply. 'And if'n Gribble is in on this poisonous scheme, he's gonna be sorry he ever tangled with us.'

There was no more to be said. The time for decisive action had arrived. Alamo cat-footed up the stairs two at a time, pausing at the top to peer through the window giving onto the saloon owner's office.

And what he witnessed only served to back up his suspicions. Bremen and Gribble were both present. And they were arguing fiercely. The gambler was sitting casually behind his desk with the agent leaning over shaking a fist. And it was Gribble who was doing most of the talking, more like shouting.

The window was partially open, enabling the eavesdropper to listen in. Wagging fingers and a scowling face accompanied the irate dialogue, proving that the devious pair had indeed been in cahoots to get rid of Huggy Johnson and steal his map. The fly in the ointment was that Bremen had decided that splitting the proceeds was not part of the plan. He denied it but the blank expression failed to impress the jabbering Gribble who accused him of wanting the entire caboodle for himself.

In keeping with a gambler's technique, Bremen was keeping a cool head. With calm deliberation he attempted to placate his irate associate. But Gribble was not swayed by the snake-oil deceit. He'd had enough. The time for talk was over. He drew a pistol from inside his jacket. Poking the gambler in the chest, he forced him to open the safe and remove the money belt containing the map.

That was when Alamo decided to intervene.

He pushed open the door and quickly stepped inside the office. 'I'll take that,' he snarled, holding out a hand.

But his revolver was pointing at Gribble who posed the immediate threat. 'Drop the hog leg, scumbag. Or eat lead.'

With the interloper's attention split, Bremen quickly seized the initiative. He threw the heavy belt at this unexpected threat. Alamo was caught wrong-footed. It struck his gun hand, sending the weapon spinning out of reach.

'You again!' Bremen growled, launching himself at the intruder. 'You're becoming a boil that needs lancing. And I'm the guy to do it.'

The two men grappled viciously, each desperately seeking to gain the edge. Fists flew. Bone on bone. Some connected while others struck thin air. A brutal combat ensued with no let up from either party. Bremen was an accomplished saloon brawler and aimed to prove it. Blood spilled from numerous cuts as they fell to the floor. Grunting and snarling like a couple of alley cats, they rolled around tearing at any exposed flesh. Chairs were sent flying. A hat stand crashed to the floor.

All the while, Gribble kept out of the way of the flying fists. Dodging this way and that, his attention was focussed on the money belt. He circled around behind the fighters to where the vital prize had landed. But the large desk was in the way.

Bremen finally managed to throw his adversary off. Scrambling to his feet, he snatched up a bottle of whiskey and flung it at the advancing target. Alamo saw it coming and dropped to the floor. Instead of connecting with flesh and bone, it smashed through the back window.

'Aaaaaaagh!' Bremen's rabid curse was more akin to that from a starving grizzly.

A foot swung at his opponent's head. Just in time, the wrangler saw the danger and swayed to one side, catching hold of the guy's boot. All his strength was needed to upend the burly combatant who crashed into a mirror, shattering it into a myriad fragments. This guy was proving to be a veritable firebrand and no easy pushover as he had assumed.

'Get the skunk, can't you?' Bremen shouted to his duped partner as he scrambled about on the floor. 'We can sort our problems out later.' But the nervous assay agent hesitated. 'Come on!' railed Bremen. 'Drop the skunk with a bullet!' The wrathful howl of ferocity concealed a note of panic.

Gribble was still holding the Starr revolver. But gun play had not been part of his agenda. The weapon was only meant to scare. All he really wanted was to gain possession of the map. He'd never killed a man, and had no intention of starting now. Such an extreme measure would only be countenanced if his own miserable life was in the balance.

Alamo took full advantage of the brief interlude to throw himself at the stunned gambler. He dragged him upright. A right followed by a left jab rattled the guy's teeth and sent him back-peddling into the hovering assay agent. Grunts of pain were the result as the two villains strove to extricate themselves from the tangled mayhem of arms and legs.

Bremen snarled as he violently flung Gribble aside. He was not finished yet. 'I've built up a good business in Buckskin. And no shiftless saddle tramp is gonna spoil my pitch.' His hand somehow found a piece of broken chair. He swung it at the wrangler's head.

Had the lethal club landed, the fight would have been over. A hand went up to deflect the fierce blow. Alamo flinched at the jolt of agony lancing up his left arm. A howl of victory cracked Bremen's blooded face. Sensing that he now had the upper hand, he stepped forward. The bludgeon was raised to deliver the final denouement as he spat out, 'You should have kept on riding after our last fracas, punk. Interfering in things that don't concern you has signed your death warrant.'

But he had left his corpulent frame open to attack. A right blow now sunk into the exposed fleshy midriff. The hard punch produced a whoosh of shocked pain like a deflated balloon. The deadly club whistled by over Alamo's head. It fell to the floor as Bremen doubled up in agony.

The wrangler shook himself, his bruised fists flexing. His left arm was still numb, useless in a brutal fight to the finish. And he was breathing heavily. The chair leg now offered him the chance to finish the contest. He grabbed it up, delivering a well-aimed blow to the gambler's head.

Silence fell as Bremen keeled over. Alamo peered around. His squinting vision was blurred and hazy from the effects of the vicious scrap. He tried shaking the mush from his brain. Only then did he notice there was no sign of Jonas Gribble. The guy had scarpered, and with him the money belt.

Now it was Alamo's turn to issue a stream of frenzied oaths.

The office was like a war zone. And in the centre of the carnage lay the supine form of Spider Bremen. Yet already he was showing signs of regaining consciousness. The victor was well aware that the fight could not have passed unheeded by those downstairs in the bar room.

A feeling of *déjà vu* flooded his lethargic brain. Once again it was time to leave. But this time he had nothing to show for the violent showdown. Gribble had disappeared with the map. And without that, he was stymied.

Alamo staggered over to the back door. His partner was coming along the rear alley leading the horses. 'Did you spot Gribble coming out of here?' he asked, hurrying down the stairs.

'I saw somebody come out and he was in a durned hurry,' replied Streater. 'But I couldn't be sure who it was. I shouted to him to stop, but the jasper ignored me. Last I saw he was spurring off around yonder bend.'

'It was Gribble,' Alamo gasped out. 'And he's taken the map. We need to get after him before Bremen recovers his senses.'

'Looks like you've had an argument with a barn door,' Streater observed, poking at his buddy's face. 'What happened up there?'

Alamo winced, pulling away. The rearrangement to his handsome features told Streater that all had not gone according to plan. But his pal had more important issues on his mind. Trouble with a capital T was still an ever-present threat to life and limb. The outcome of the saloon altercation would have to wait.

And another danger now presented itself.

TEN

FLIGHT

At the far end of the alley six men appeared. And they were led by Clay Bowman.

'The cat is out of the bag now,' groaned Streater, jabbing a finger at the unexpected arrivals. 'Somebody must have spotted us talking to Jane and raised the alarm.'

The men stopped when they saw the escaping felons. Deputy Wardle was standing beside the sheriff. He instantly eyeballed the two men who had made a fool of him. Here was his chance to reclaim the initiative along with his tarnished reputation. He jumped forward.

The blunt call to surrender was accompanied by a waving six gun. 'Drop the hardware,' he shouted. 'You critters are under arrest. And this time I'll chain you both to the hoosegow floor.'

'Not if'n I can help it,' Alamo shouted back. He loosed off a couple of slugs over the posse's head. Everybody except Wardle leapt for cover.

The deputy was madder than a cornered sidewinder. Without thinking he triggered off a whole chamber of slugs at the two ne'er-do-wells. Unfortunately for Hank Wardle, in the fervour of the moment he had overestimated the range of a hand gun. And they dropped well short.

Alamo let out a hoarse bout of guffawing. 'You'll have to do a sight better than that, tin star, if'n you're gonna catch us guys.'

The rash fit of heckling only served to incense the poor guy even further. He was hopping about like a Mexican jumping bean.

'I'll get you rats if'n it's the last thing I do,' he railed impotently, struggling to reload the pistol. In any other circumstances it would have elicited a bout of hilarity from the watching posse men.

The sheriff now stepped in to take control. 'Don't be such a durned idiot,' the irate lawman admonished his deputy. 'Ain't you learned nothing? Pistols are no use at this range.' His disparaging remark caused the tarnished deputy to flush. 'All of you, round to the front. And this time use your rifles. That's the only way we'll drop 'em before they leave town.'

The fracas with Bremen in the saloon had not passed unnoticed in the main bar of the Rim Rock. Slickback Charlie, the 'keep, had heard the racket but feared to intervene alone. Discarding his apron, he had hurried next door to the Rib-Eye Diner where the boss's two bodyguards were enjoying a hearty lunch.

'Come on, you two, the boss needs our help,' he shouted at the startled duo. 'That assay agent is causing trouble. There's a right shindig going on up in the office. Didn't you hear all the shooting?'

Haikon spat out a lurid curse along with a mouthful of potato. 'Ain't nothing strange about guns going off in this town. Anyway, we're busy,' he grumbled, continuing to fill his face. 'Can't you handle it?'

'No chance. I'm a bartender, not a gunslinger,' he protested. 'That's what you guys are paid for. Now come on!'

Reluctantly the duo was forced to abandon their unfinished meal. All three men returned to the saloon and hastened upstairs to ascertain the source of the affray. Bremen was struggling to his feet when they entered the office. His head was throbbing. But his fury at having been bested by two no-good drifters eclipsed any pain from his injuries.

Meanwhile the two fugitives knew that they needed to quit Buckskin *rapido* before the shooting got serious and somebody was hurt. They mounted up and swung round, darting up a connecting passageway and onto the main street. With spurs dug in they hurtled off, zig-zagging to throw off the posse's aim. Heads were bent low over the necks of their horses to further present a reduced target.

Sheriff Bowman and his men had tried to cut off their escape. The deep-throated roar of half a dozen rifles found bullets whistling past the ears of the two galloping runaways like angry hornets. But the strategy had worked. None found their mark. A split second later they swung round a corner at the head of the main street and disappeared from view.

The crackle of gunfire saw Bremen rushing down the corridor to the front veranda. But he was too late. By then, Alamo and his pard were out of sight. Down below in the street, Bowman was urging his men to get mounted to chase after the alleged killers. And this time they would not escape. Bremen threw a snarled cuss at the stoical lawman before swinging on his heel and returning to the office. He would deal with those wranglers later.

What made him more agitated than ever was the discovery that the map had disappeared. And so had Jonas Gribble. The conclusion was obvious. During the brawl, the conniving rat must have seen an opportunity and taken it. The gang boss's temple then furrowed in thought. Or was it that crazy cayuse cracker? But it was only a momentary aberration. The pair had been too busy knocking seven bells out of each other. He was never given the chance to seize the map. No, it had to be Gribble.

So what to do now? Quick thinking had made him a successful gambler and wheeler-dealer. The sharp brain now got to work. And once again it came up trumps. There was still the old miner's daughter. She was known to have taken up residence in the dead man's cabin. Her father must have shown her the map. She might not know the exact location, but was bound to have some idea of the general location. That was all Bremen needed to know.

He would then be able to suss out Gribble's trail. Hunting the Judas down would be a simple matter with the help of Squint Haikon who was known to be an expert tracker. All this was filtering through Bremen's devious mind while his men were idly pondering over the devastation inside the office.

He called Haikon to one side. 'Get the boys together and load up with plenty of guns and ammo. We have work to do.'

The hard case grinned. This was what he liked to hear. Anything concerned with gun play was like nectar to the gods for the hard-boiled gunman. 'That's the kind of work we cotton to. Ain't that right, Idaho?' The lazy eye twitched wildly as Haikon slung a knowing wink at his sidekick. 'So where are we going, boss?'

'Jonas Gribble must have somehow found out that he wasn't part of the deal.' The gambler was not listening. A purple cast indicative of bubbling anger suffused the perverted features. 'I don't know how. But when I find out, the skunk who blabbed is gonna wish his mama had kept her drawers on.'

The two bodyguards visibly blanched. Pete Weller threw a nervous look at his sidekick. It was on account of their selling the gold nuggets to Gribble that the wily assay agent had cottoned to their source. Lucky for them, nothing seemed to have been mentioned during the confrontation.

And that's how both men intended it to stay. An unspoken agenda flitted between the two men. First chance they got, Jonas Gribble would be dog meat. No opportunity could be allowed for the turncoat to reveal their part in his discovery of Bremen's double-cross.

The whole of the gambler's concentration was stewing on revenge. So he failed to heed the shifty looks passed between the two guilty bodyguards. 'But first we have to secure that map,' he went on, 'or at least find out where the secret mine is located. And Johnson's daughter is gonna solve that problem.'

Haikon replied with a quick nod gesturing for Weller to follow him down to the livery barn. They both heaved sighs of relief that their part in the fiasco had not come under close scrutiny. The boss appeared to have forgotten about those nuggets he gave them. And they sure weren't about to remind him.

The saloon owner's final orders were for Slickback Charlie. 'While we're away, you clear up this mess. And not a word to anyone about where we've gone.'

'Sure thing, boss. You can count on me.'

Bremen responded with a curt nod. 'Good man. When this is over, there'll be hefty bonuses all round. And I'm gonna make Gribble suffer before I kill the rat.'

Spider Bremen presented an outward aura of confidence. But his guts were churning. In the space of a few days, his whole enterprise seemed to be falling apart. First the argument with Gribble, then the fight with that nosey wrangler. But worst of all, was the loss of the vital map which he needed to register his claim as the legitimate owner of the mine. Without it he was up shit creek with nothing to show for all this trouble.

A hard-nosed tough, Bremen had operated in some

of the toughest bergs in the West. Wichita immediately sprang to mind. A hell's-a-poppin' cow town described as being 'wild and woolly where anything goes.' But success as a high-roller had made him soft. Easy living with others to do his dirty work had taken its toll. The effects of the violent confrontation were evident on his bruised face.

The message was clear. Buckskin had become too hot for Spider Bremen's continued good health and prosperity. But he was not leaving without the Lost Dutchman's secret cache. Then it would be goodbye, Arizona and hello, California where he owned a small piece of land in the San Fernando Valley. A couple of Mexicans had been looking after the place since he had acquired it a year previously.

That high principled sheriff was becoming too much of a problem, a thorn in Bremen's side. Rockwall was a fitting name for Clay Bowman. Sure, he could have Haikon and Weller gun the bastard down. But that was asking for trouble. Bowman was a well-respected fixture in Buckskin, not to mention the whole county.

ELEVEN

BAD DECISION

With her boss and all the other employees otherwise engaged, Galloping Jane decided now was the time to pursue her own investigation. Only Slickback Charlie the bartender remained in the saloon bar. And he was busy clearing up after the hurried exit when the shooting started.

The woman's normal truculent manner as depicted by her garish nickname would have to be curbed if her objective was to be achieved. Great care was accordingly exercised as she sidled up the stairs. Charlie continued with his task, totally unaware of her clandestine plot. Reaching the first storey, Jane realized that she had been holding her breath. The heaving bosom lurched as she released a deep sigh.

At the end of the corridor, Bremen's office door stood wide open. In the furore following the recent showdown and the flight of the perpetrators, the boss had clearly abandoned his usual caution. Panic at the challenge to his dominion must have set in.

The woman's face broke in a mirthless smile. But Jane knew she did not have much time to find evidence of Bremen's chicanery. Forged land deals, stolen mining claim certificates, decks of marked cards and much more. All would be tucked away inside his safe. Hopefully, in his hurry to chase after those troublesome wranglers, he would have left it unlocked.

Caution tempered the urge to hurry as she entered the hallowed private quarters. And there it was, staring her in the face. Large eyes popped with delight when the sturdy door swung open. The woman had no idea what she was searching for. All she knew was that Spider Bremen was an assiduous record keeper. Every transaction was noted down in a ledger. He ran the whole enterprise in the manner of a ship's captain. It was his Teutonic ancestry coming to the fore.

Had he been aware of how much Jane knew about his criminal empire, Bremen would have rubbed her out long ago. Being a canny madam in charge of the erotic side of the saloon's business made her privy to a host of under-handed skulduggery.

A guy was at his most vulnerable when full of liquor with his pants down. All manner of secrets were then divulged with no recollections of the imprudence the following day. That was how Galloping Jane had learned about Bremen's illicit deals. Had he treated her better, maybe things would have been different. But the guy was nought but a vainly avaricious hoodlum who deserved to be taken down. And she was the gal to do it.

So intent was Jane on rummaging through the contents of the safe that the arrival of Slickback went unnoticed. Always eager to keep well in with the boss, Charlie had abandoned his bar room task to tackle the wrecked office. Catching the saloon madam red-handed with her hands in the safe was bound to raise his stature in Bremen's eyes. The gambler was ruthless with those who crossed him. But there was no denying that he was generous to those who served him well.

Charlie tip-toed gingerly across the carpeted floor. For a guy of corpulent proportions he moved with surprising lightness. A thick arm encircled her neck as he dragged her back.

Jane elicited a choking scream. But a natural feline instinct for survival immediately kicked in. Working in a cat house was a guaranteed way to toughen up the most gentle of dames. And Galloping Jane Channing had never regarded herself as anything less than resilient. You had to be tough in her profession, especially as a madam. Most men regarded her sort as barely human, bodies to be used and discarded. Only on the rarest of occasions would a real man come along who displayed care and concern.

Such a man was Kid Streater. The thought of helping him and his buddy out made her all the more determined to resist.

Snarling like a cornered tiger, she struggled fiercely.

Sharp nails raked her assailant's face, drawing thin lines of red. Now it was the barman's turn to cry out. But he hung on, his greater strength forcing her to the ground. Indeed, the woman's animalistic defiance resurrected a latent sadistic streak.

He slugged her hard with a bunch fist. The solid thwack caught Jane high on the forehead. It stunned her, giving the brutish bartender his chance to gain the upper hand. The oily leer matched the guy's mussed up hair. Another harsh backhander effectively terminated the one-sided clash.

Charlie stumbled to his feet, gasping for breath. A hissing wince sizzled through tight lips when a careless paw touched his injuries. That precipitated a swinging boot into Jane's ribs.

'You'll pay dearly for this, harlot,' he rasped, quickly securing the woman's hands behind her back using her own hair ribbons. 'I'll have the boss hand you over to me once he's had his fun. You won't be laughing then.' Jane was dragged to her feet and violently pushed down the corridor. 'The root cellar will soon crush your spirit.'

The woman remained silent. Yet inside she was quaking. 'I was only after getting what's owed me,' she remonstrated, desperately trying to break free. 'Spider hasn't paid me in a month. I need that money to pay my landlady.'

Charlie cuffed her round the head. 'Don't insult the boss by calling him that name. He don't like it. You can explain your lame excuses to him when he gets back.'

But Jane was not going down into that fetid dungeon without a struggle. The barman was forced to summon help. 'Over here quick, Wishbone,' he called out to a swamper. 'Give me a hand with this she-devil. I caught her robbing the boss's safe.'

'That ain't true!' But the panic-stricken denial fell on deaf ears.

Grabbing an arm each, the two men man-handled her through a door at the rear. A hard shove sent her tumbling down the last few steps into the subterranean chamber. The saloon had begun life trading in farm produce. It was one of the few premises in Buckskin with a cellar. That was its prime selling point when the original business ceased operations. A cool cellar offered the ideal place to store beer barrels.

It had now found an extra use as a prison. With no windows and a solid door, escape was impossible. Jane shuddered. And it was not from the chilly air. She was scared witless. Only Slickback Charlie and the thin weed of a swamper called Wishbone knew she was there.

The door slammed shut and Jane was left alone in the harsh doom-laden silence. Another tremble riddled her frame. Tears ran down her smudged cheeks. The silence was bad enough. But more disconcerting was the pitch blackness. The place still stunk of rotting vegetables. Her guts lurched uncontrollably as the contents of her stomach were vomited up. How worse could things get? Plenty if Spider Bremen had his way. All she could hope for now was that somehow the Kid would come riding to her rescue. Just like those knights in shining armour she read about as a youngster.

But for the moment Galloping Jane was going nowhere.

Up above, Spider Bremen had just returned from arranging his trek into the Mescal Mountains. Slickback Charlie was not slow in acquainting him with the beer cellar's latest occupant. Bremen cussed out loud, a balled fist pounding the bar top. He was like a man possessed. Was everybody's hand against him?

Yet ever the devious racketeer and gambler, Bremen was quick to recognize the captive woman's usefulness as a hostage. He knew that Streater and the madam were old acquaintances, much more if what Charlie had learned was true. The Kid was sweet on her. If things did not go according to plan, Galloping Jane would be his ace up the sleeve.

'Keep your eye on that treacherous cow, Charlie,' the saloon boss ordered. 'I'm holding you responsible for her still being here when I return.' A withering look told the barman in no uncertain terms that dire consequences would be his bonus should things go awry.

The barman blanched. 'You got my word on it, boss. Jane won't be galloping off any place while I'm in charge,' he assured Bremen.

Squint Haikon stuck his head in the door of the saloon. 'We're all set, boss. The boys are mounted up outside. And I've fixed up a pack mule with provisions and extra ammo.'

Bremen joined him. 'OK, boys, let's ride.'

*

Heading in the opposite direction, the two fugitives were anxious to escape the fury of the law that was now hot on their trail. They were bent low over the necks of the galloping horses, urging them to full speed. The wind whipped their hat brims flat. But that frenetic pace could not be maintained indefinitely. After half an hour, the mounts were beginning to tire. Alamo knew they couldn't keep it up much longer.

He chanced a look behind. The rising dust cloud informed him that the posse were overhauling them. Bowman had clearly commandeered fresh mounts.

'We have to give these guys the slip,' he shouted to his buddy above the roar of pounding hoofs. 'But I'm plumb out of ideas.' The recent fracas had numbed his brain, but not his body which ached all over.

Kid Streater's brow furrowed with anxiety as he silently considered the unholy mess they had landed themselves with. This business was indeed getting mighty serious. But for now, thwarting that posse was imperative.

'That group of trees up ahead,' he called back. 'Soon as we're in among them, pull off the trail and hide up while the posse goes past. They'll only figure out we've tricked them when they come out at the far side. That will give us some breathing space to find a different route before they've realized what's happened.'

Alamo nodded. It was a good plan. Indeed it was the only plan.

Five minutes later, the welcoming shelter of the clump

of palos verdes embraced them.

'Those dudes are about ten minutes behind. That should give us time to get well under cover,' Streater announced. 'In the dim light they won't notice that our hoof prints have disappeared.'

Alamo offered a half smile. The effort was painful. 'By then we'll have split the breeze and disappeared.' A family of quail chirped out what sounded like a positive response to the subterfuge. 'Those guys certainly agree with your plan,' he quipped.

'Now all we can do is hold our breath and hope it works,' came back the nerve-edged retort as Streater dismounted, grabbing hold of a fallen branch. 'Just to make sure, I'll rub out our prints,' he added as Alamo led their mounts into the heart of the wooded enclave. 'Can't be too careful where posses are concerned.'

Their recent altercation with Rockwall Bowman was proof of that assertion. Minutes passed slowly as the two men waited in the verdant screen of trees. Heaving chests told of the tension building. The rustle of dried leaves akin to a thousand mice scampering overhead only served to rack up the tight atmosphere. Any moment now and their fate would be determined.

Was it to be a reprieve and the chance to clear their names? Or were they destined to dance with the devil in Hell?

All too soon, the steady drub of shod horses assailed their ears. Louder, ever louder the pounding thud drew closer. Then suddenly, the passing flash of bodies could be seen through the dense canopy of undergrowth. Alamo strained his ears. Was that a slackening in pace he detected? No, there was no let up in the rhythmic beat to indicate the posse had spotted their diversion. He could breathe easy again. For now.

'Looks like your plan worked, pard,' he gasped out, complimenting his buddy. 'Let's get back on the trail pronto. Those jaspers won't take long to figure out they've been hoodwinked.'

'What do you have in mind?' Streater asked as he quickly mounted up.

'We can back track aways before branching off. Then head for the Mescals to where Freda Johnson is holed up. My bet is that Bremen and his gang will try and force her hand somehow. She's the only person who will have any notion as to where her pa discovered the Lost Dutchman.'

'Do you know the location of her cabin?' Streater enquired.

'She told me whilst you were getting the horses when we last met up in Tonto Canyon. It's up a draw near some landmark called War Bonnet Rock on the west side of the Mescals. Shouldn't be too hard to find.'

TWELVE

DEADLY DEMONSTRATION

Much as he would have loved to rest up some place, Alamo knew that was not an option. Too much was now at stake if they were to clear their names. So he set a course for the distant Mescals.

True to its colourful appendage, the landmark rock was indeed shaped like an Indian headdress. And it was easy to pinpoint. Only a blind man could miss such an outstanding prominence. Hank Wardle had also let slip the information about the landmark while drinking in the Rim Rock. The ever-watchful Slickback Charlie had passed it on to Spider Bremen.

As the deputy sheriff and his posse had spurred off to the east in search of the two escaped 'killers', the gang of gold seekers were headed in the opposite direction.

No time could be wasted if Jonas Gribble was to be prevented from securing the hidden gold mine. Accordingly they cut across the country, making a beeline for the War

Bonnet. No attempt at subterfuge was contemplated as they swung off into the adjacent draw. Caution had been thrown to the wind. Bremen knew that the dame had chosen to live here alone so he had no fear of meeting any serious resistance.

The eight riders thundered along the draw, splashing across the creek just as the girl was drawing water. She was completely taken by surprise.

Normally a cautious girl, Freda Johnson had become careless. Only the two wranglers and Sheriff Bowman knew where she was holed up. Surely none of them would have spoken out. But she hadn't reckoned with the loose-lipped neglect of Hank Wardle. And now she would pay the price for her folly. The rifle she always kept nearby had been left in the cabin.

Desperation lent speed to her recovery. The ugly leers told their own grim tale. These men clearly meant her harm. Discarding the bucket she dashed back towards the cabin. But her long legs were no match for a galloping horse. Squint Haikon caught her up and jabbed his boot heel into her back. The girl was pitched forward into the dirt. He and his buddy quickly grabbed her. Freda snapped and snarled like a tethered bear. But she stood no chance against the two burly critters.

'Let me go, you big ape,' she yelled out. 'There's nothing in the cabin worth stealing if it's an easy snatch you're after.'

Her feline resistance only incited sardonic amusement from the gang. Churlish guffaws accompanied the girl's feeble efforts to break free. Bremen dismounted and stood in front of the snarling minx. His mirthless smile and apathetic demeanour soon brought home the notion that further resistance was futile. Her narrow shoulders slumped, the pretty head drooping.

'That's better,' the gang boss derisively applauded. 'Things will be a sight easier if'n you co-operate.'

Freda gave the remark a quizzical frown. 'I don't know what you mean.' Her proud head lifted. The shock of auburn hair flicked to indicate the disdain she held against these bullying braggarts.

But Bremen was through playing the waiting game. Every minute wasted was assisting Gribble in getting away with the loot. Once again the laissez-faire manner instantly changed. A black scowl clouding the hard face was made all the more sinister by the bruising from the recent fight.

'It ain't what's in the cabin that concerns me,' he growled, jabbing a finger at the girl's head. 'It's what you're holding up there. If'n you want to be difficult, there are ways and means of inducing co-operation. But they ain't pleasant.'

He signalled to one of his men. A lumbering Indian half-breed stepped forward.

'Cherokee Joe here is an expert with a knife.' The remark was casually delivered. 'Show the lady what you can do, Joe.'

The Indian attempted a smile. It emerged as a sour grimace. In the blink of an eye, the deadly blade was palmed. A few deft swings aimed at impressing his buddies followed. The performance received a round of applause and was followed by a thrusting slice. Freda gasped as the flashing steel ripped through the bandanna encircling her neck. The two sections fell apart with nary a drop of blood spilt.

'See what I mean,' Bremen drawled once again, adopting an affable persona. 'He learnt his technique skinning beaver hides. But he's equally at home with human prey. That head band is from the back of a guy who played me false last year. He didn't enjoy the experience. But Joe certainly did.'

Bremen stood eyeing the girl, allowing the import of the half breed's demonstration to sink in. 'And he ain't particular as to who he practises on, if'n you get my drift.'

'What is it you want from me?' Freda croaked, still totally in ignorance of this loathsome creature's wishes. 'I have nothing of any value here.'

'Don't play the innocent with me, girly,' the gang leader scowled. 'You know exactly what I want to know. The location of the Lost Dutchman.'

'But I don't have the map,' Freda remonstrated. 'It was stolen from my father when he was callously shot down.' A granite-like glint of hate speared the gang boss. 'And my guess is that it was you and this bunch of cowards that killed him.'

She made to break free of the toughs holding her. Sharp claws lunged at the scowling face of Spider Bremen. But her captors' grip was firm. The instinctive reaction for vengeance was easily quashed.

'The old goat must have told you where the mine was located even if'n you never saw the map,' growled Bremen, stepping forward and backhanding her across the face. 'Now talk, damn you. Or Joe here will dig it out of you.'

Blood dribbled from the girl's cut mouth. Her will to resist was flagging. The clock was ticking and Bremen was impatient to leave. A quick jerk of the head to Cherokee Joe saw the red man flexing his knife as he stepped forward.

That was the moment Freda knew that the game was over. And she had lost.

'All right, all right,' she moaned. 'I'll tell you what I know. But it ain't much. The map was stolen before I could study it properly. All I know is that the mine is in the Superstition Mountains at the head of Castle Canyon. Look out for a rock called the Scorpion's Tail. The mine is somewhere near that.' Her head fell onto her chest, abject misery threatening to overwhelm her.

'Is it easy to find?' broke in Squint Haikon.

'I haven't had the time to go up there,' Freda muttered. 'I only know what I've already told you.'

'Now that wasn't so hard, was it?' The relieved gang boss smirked. His next remark was for the Indian and a guy called Scab Lakin. 'You fellas stay here and keep Miss Johnson company. We can't have her wandering off and raising the alarm now, can we? OK, boys, let's ride. We've got a gold mine to investigate.' A final warning sent shivers of dread racing down Freda's spine. 'And if'n this turns out to be a wild goose chase, you know what to expect. Joe here is feeling a mite peeved at being denied his fun.'

'How about taking the girl's wagon, boss?' Pete Weller suggested. 'There could be a heap of ready bagged gold up there just waiting to be carried off.'

'Good thinking, Idaho.' Bremen nodded approvingly. 'You can drive.'

THIRTEEN

THE DUTCHMAN DELIVERS

The Superstition Mountains ran parallel to the Mescals which were on their northern flank. Separating the two ranges was a broad stretch of wilderness called Tortilla Flats. Jonas Gribble had studied the map closely once he was clear of Buckskin. A thorough check of his back trail involving numerous stops had satisfied the robber that he was not being followed.

The sound of gunfire had carried easily on the light desert breeze. It brought a satisfied leer to his bloated features. About time those interfering cowpokes suffered their justly deserved comeuppance. Although it was Spider Bremen whom he was most intent on avoiding.

Jubilation that the famous mystery of the lost mine had finally been solved overshadowed any trepidation that his skulduggery would be foiled. After all, he was now in possession of the vital map indicating its source, the only person who knew how to find it. Even more so was the fact that it was so close to where he had been living all this time.

Who would have believed that the Lost Dutchman's mine was no more than a half day's ride from Buckskin?

Over the years, numerous searches of the Superstitions by a host of intrepid adventurers had revealed nothing. Many bold adventurers had entered the mysterious region, never to be heard from again. Gribble harboured no worries on that score. Huggy Johnson's map identified the exact spot.

Gribble chuckled to himself. 'Ha, ha, ha!' he burbled inanely. 'Bad luck, old man. The mine now belongs to Jonas Gribble. And he ain't about to share the secret with anyone else.'

Once over the Mescal Range, the trail dropped steadily through a stretch of boulder strewn country to an uneven sprawl of wilderness dotted with sage brush and the ubiquitous saguaro cactus. Other cactus growth also thrived in the arid land with cholla and prickly pear pre-dominant. Another two hours of travel across Tortilla Flats brought him to the surging buffer of the Superstitions. His heart began to race at the thought of what he would soon uncover. Castle Canyon with its line of serrated ramparts and entrance akin to a medieval fortress stood proud and solid, clearly visible from afar.

Once inside the narrowing ravine, Gribble checked the map for the umpteenth time. The landmark that supposedly held the clue to uncovering the mine was named as the Scorpion's Tail. A penned depiction gave it the appearance of a curved fang thrusting out of the sandy wasteland. The reprobate spurred towards the top end of the constricted gorge, keeping a wary eye open for the outlandish marker. Castle Canyon opened out into a circular amphitheatre at his head. And there it was, just like the map had indicated.

So where was the mine? No information was included on the map as to the exact site of the fabled hoard. Perhaps that was why nobody had ever found it and lived to tell the tale. They had died in this god forsaken wasteland, driven crazy by fruitless exploration that revealed nothing but rock and sand rather than the hypnotic allure of the yellow peril.

It had been Huggy Johnson's intention to mark that vital spot only when he reached Phoenix and the Land Registry Office. That precautionary measure was for just such an occurrence as Gribble now faced.

Dark shadows were crawling across the arid landscape by the time Gribble realized the search was going to take longer than anticipated. Although loath to spend a night in the hauntingly sinister enclave, he was not about to quit the scene without his reward. He was accordingly forced to hunker down under a saddle blanket with only the baleful howling of coyotes for company.

Sleep did not come easily to the cringing charlatan, his turbulent thoughts reflecting on all the things that could go wrong. Nightmares periodically invaded his personal domain. More than once he awoke in a fear-induced sweat. It was with much relief that the false dawn broke across the scalloped moulding of the Canyon rim. Jonas Gribble heartily concluded that the Superstitions had been aptly named.

He stretched the stiffness from tight muscles as the sun rose above the skyline. Slowly it lifted, filling the enclosed basin with heat-nourished light. Higher, ever higher it rose into the early morning firmament. But at the same time a singular phenomenon was taking shape. Shadows of rock formations spread their tentacles across the bottomland.

One particular spectacle caught Gribble's attention. The sun-kissed shadow from the Scorpion's Tail scuttled across the ground just like its namesake. And it was pointing directly towards a crack in the rock wall on the west side of the arena. The assay agent's staring eyes followed its progress. The strange occurrence only lasted thirty seconds before it faded away.

The excited prospector leapt onto his horse and urged it up the loose slope towards the foot of the cliff face where the crack was more obvious. Large boulders forced him to tackle the final section on foot. Sheer exhilaration at the anticipation of what he was about to uncover lent strength to the unaccustomed physical exertion.

A final scramble and he was over the lip. The bottom section of the cliff was guarded by a natural wall five feet high. Over hundreds of years loose rock fragments had tumbled from the heights above and formed a natural barrier behind which could be seen the dark entrance to a cave. From the base of the amphitheatre it was completely hidden from view. Only up close was the opening visible to the naked eye. No wonder it had remained undiscovered for so long.

Beady peepers gaped wide. At last he had located the Lost Dutchman's mine. How the old prospector had chanced upon such a remote out-of-the-way setting did not trouble Jonas Gribble. An avaricious leer cracked the blotchy countenance.

With slow deliberation, he climbed over the barrier and moved towards the hallowed portal, hardly daring to breathe in case the bubble burst and it turned out to be another piece of surreal fantasy. There he stopped, swallowing down a nervous gulp. The entrance was barely more than a narrow fissure, a natural split in the rock wall.

Finally he stepped inside. A tallow brand had been left by the previous visitor which had to be Huggy Johnson. Gribble scratched a vesta on the roughly hewn wall and ignited it. There was no need to move any deeper into the mine. Here were laid out bags of what must contain the mine's bounty, namely high grade gold nuggets. Old Huggy had clearly been hard at work. And it was all for the benefit of Jonas Gribble. And doubtless there was much more to be dug out further inside the mine.

'Much obliged, old timer.' The thief tipped his hat in mock acknowledgement. 'You won't regret your generosity.' A mirthless cackle echoed around the stark chamber.

Trembling hands then delved into one of the bags and nervously removed a sample. A cry of blissful ecstasy issued from the flapping maw. The tallow brand illuminated the treasure trove in all its mesmeric glory. For a whole minute Jonas Gribble stared at the fabulous lump of El Dorado. It sure looked like the real thing. But a proper check was needed before he could be certain this was not some devilish trick, a cunning ploy to trap the unwary.

He quickly stepped back outside into the sunlight and studied the nugget with his eyeglass. His breath quickened along with a stampeding heartbeat. There was no doubt. This was indeed the Dutchman's long lost hoard.

There was far too much in the cave for one man to carry on a horse. The greedy assay agent stuffed his pockets with a number of suitable nuggets. Hefting one of the sacks onto his shoulder, he went outside, intending to fill his saddle bags. The horse was chewing on some grass halfway down the boulder-strewn slope.

Once the first bag was full, the sack was discarded. There was still enough room in the other for one more. Then he would leave and ride straight to Phoenix and register the mine in his name.

For the second time he scrambled up the rough slope and disappeared into the mine.

Bremen and his men had made good time. The girl's rather sketchy description had proved to be unusually accurate. No time had been wasted in fruitless searching for the entrance to Castle Canyon. And once inside the main bastion, the Scorpion's Tail had stood out like a sore thumb. However, if it hadn't been for Gribble's horse tethered halfway up the facing slope, the actual location of the mine would have proved distinctly tricky, if not impossible to find.

'The rat must be inside the mine. It'll be up there someplace,' Bremen muttered. 'Don't matter where. We'll split up and circle around to catch him when he comes out.' A biting chuckle, brittle and macabre, told of dire consequences to follow. 'Squint and Idaho, head up that gully on the left. You others go right. That way he won't have a chance to escape. I'll stay by the wagon to keep an eye on things.'

Before the men could disperse, he laid down a specific proviso. 'Make sure to bring that cheating waster down here. He's gonna suffer good before I put a bullet in his shiftless hide.'

Haikon shot a knowing look at his buddy as they scuttled off. The two bodyguards made sure they were in the vanguard as the men dispersed. As a result they were in position close to the rocky parapet when the assay agent emerged. So intent was he on watching his footing that he failed to heed the two jaspers who stepped out from behind a rock.

'I'll take that, Gribble,' Haikon barked. His gun was deliberately still resting in its holster. 'The boss wants words with you. So don't try anything stupid.' He stepped forward, hand held out.

For a brief second, the agent was nonplussed, stunned by this sudden threat to his plans. Staring eyes focussed on the bodyguard, unable to comprehend what was happening. His mouth flapped. 'Wh-what's ...'

'Just hand over the gold and come quietly, if'n you know what's good for you,' Haikon repeated, knowing full well the scumbag would try to retaliate.

A hint of a smile creased Gribble's face on seeing his adversary without a gun. No thought was given to the obvious conclusion that this buzzard was not operating alone. 'Nobody is going to stop me registering this find in my name.'

The sneering retort found the agent reaching for his own pistol. It lifted halfway out of the holster when a bullet struck him in the back. Total surprise registered on the ashen features as he reeled like a drunken man. Another shot finished the job as Pete Weller appeared from nowhere. The Idaho gunslinger cheekily blew the smoke from his revolver barrel.

'That gets rid of him,' Weller said. 'And it sure saves us a heap of grief having to explain why we sold him those stones. But Spider ain't gonna be too pleased.'

Haikon shrugged off the insignificant detail. 'We'll just tell him the truth. The guy refused to hand over the map and drew his gun. What alternative was there?'

With that problem out of the way. Squint Haikon searched Gribble's body while his pal checked the horse.

'Here's the map,' Haikon said.

'And these saddle bags are chock full of gold nuggets,' Weller exclaimed in surprise. 'There must be a fortune still up in the mine waiting to be loaded onto the wagon. We're gonna be rich, Squint.'

Broad smiles wreathed the stubble-coated faces of the two gunslingers. They left the blood stained corpse for the scavengers to feast upon as they led the horse down to where Bremen was waiting. They were soon joined by the other members of the gang. Haikon's justification for Gribble's death was grudgingly accepted by Bremen. In truth he was more taken with getting back the all-important map to secure his own claim to the mine.

'OK boys, let's see what we have up there.' His avaricious gaze flicked to the distant crack from which Gribble had recently emerged. 'Then we can start loading the wagon.'

FOURTEEN

STING IN THE TAIL

Todd Heffridge and his buddy pushed their horses hard. Like those before them, they encountered no difficulty locating War Bonnet Rock. It was when the cabin hove into view that uncertainty etched its ambiguous outline across the frowning countenance.

What were three horses doing outside the cabin? He could have accepted one as belonging to Freda. Did another two mean that she had visitors? He drew to a halt behind a copse of palos verdes and carefully studied the surrounding environs. Nothing moved to indicate all was not as it should be. But Alamo Todd was by nature a suspicious guy. His partner picked up on his hesitation.

'I see what's bugging you, pard,' Streater concurred. 'You figure that's Bremen up there holding the girl hostage.'

Alamo shook his head. 'Not with only two men. My bet

is that he's forced her to reveal the source of the gold and left those two jaspers on guard.' His mouth tightened, a hard gleam auguring badly for those who might have harmed the girl which he voiced in a guttural hiss. 'She better be all right.'

Streater sensed that his buddy was all set to barge up there, such was his anger. 'Don't let your heart rule your head, boy,' the older bronc man cautioned. 'We need to think this out. Charge in like a pair of crazy fools and we're done for. And there's no telling what will happen to the girl.'

'You're right, Kid,' Alamo accepted, curbing his impatience. 'I just can't bear the thought of her being up there in the hands of those bastards.'

'Me neither, so this is the plan,' came the firm decision. 'If'n we take 'em from either side of the cabin in one synchronized swoop, the surprise will give us the edge to put the boot in firmly.'

'Sounds good to me, buddy,' Alamo concurred. 'I'll slide around to the back while you sneak up close to the front door.' He was checking his revolver as he added with a note of concern, 'But how we gonna make certain that Freda don't get hurt?'

'When I'm ready listen out for that coyote howl you reckon sounds like a strangled turkey,' suggested Streater.

Alamo chuckled. 'Turkey, coyote, buzzard, who cares? Don't matter what it sounds like so long as we do this together.'

'I'll give you enough time to get in position before

142

I give the signal. You should hear movement inside the main room as the guy comes to investigate. Once he opens the door ...'

'Showtime! And make every bullet count.'

They shook hands then departed in opposite directions. Keeping to the cover of rocks and undergrowth, no difficulty was encountered in manoeuvring into position. Alamo found the back door unbolted. These guys were clearly not expecting any adverse company. Quiet as the proverbial church mouse, he crept across the back room. With an ear to the door of the twin-roomed cabin, he listened intently.

'How's about you rustling up some grub, girl, I'm starving,' came the blunt order from one of the sentinels.

The scraping of a chair followed as Freda appeared to obey. That was a stroke of luck as she would be out of the firing line when the action started. Moments later the low yet insistent refrain penetrated the cabin walls.

'What's that?' came the puzzled query from Cherokee Joe.

'A coyote must have strayed too close,' grunted Scab Lakin. 'I'll soon scare it off with a load of buckshot.'

A clumping of boots was followed moments later by the front door creaking open. Alamo sucked in a deep lungful of air and slammed through the connecting door. Hawkish eyes picked out the sprawled figure of a half-breed picking dirt from his nails with a huge knife.

Freda was on the far side of the room beside the stove. Her impulsive response was a startled scream of

143

terror. Then she saw who had barged in and immediately dropped to the floor. The unexpected intrusion caught the Indian completely by surprise. He made to raise the deadly blade. The revolver in Alamo's hand bucked three times. Each shot found its mark in the breed's chest.

'Stay down! Don't move!' he hollered at the girl as he dashed across to the front door. His gun panned the immediate vicinity, ready to dispense more death-dealing persuasion. But he need not have worried. Kid Streater was straddling Lakin's body. The stocky thug would not be causing them any further problems. A knife blade was buried in the guy's chest up to the hilt.

'Reckon that was a first class operation old Robert E. Lee himself would have been proud of,' he eulogized, dragging the knife free and squaring his shoulders smugly.

Unlike his pal who had been too young, Streater had been a foot soldier during the Civil War. Being on the losing side had clearly not hindered his capacity to deliver a decisive blow to the enemy.

'You could be right, buddy,' Alamo accepted. 'Maybe we're in the wrong profession.' Then he remembered that Freda Johnson's life had been in the balance during their attack. He hurried back into the cabin where the girl was crouched down beside the stove.

She was shaking like a leaf from nervous tension. The death of her father followed by her incarceration and the threatening presence of Cherokee Joe were bad enough. A brutal gun battle within her own domain was the final straw. It was all too much. Tears flowed. Desperately she clung to the man who had saved her and now held her tight. He stroked her hair, murmuring heartfelt endearments into her ear.

Meanwhile Streater boiled some water. Strong hot coffee laced with a liberal shot of whiskey was his answer to all such distressing predicaments.

A half hour later with the bodies removed from sight, Freda was feeling much better. Eager to go in pursuit of Spider Bremen and the rest of his gang, it took a heap of earnest beseeching on Todd Heffridge's part to persuade her otherwise.

'You can help us more by going back to Buckskin and bringing the sheriff to Castle Canyon,' he implored the feisty girl. 'The Kid and I can hold them off in the neck of the ravine if'n what your pa told you was right.'

The girl nodded, recognizing that her anger was over-riding good judgement. 'He specifically said that a couple of men with rifles positioned in the entrance could hold off an army.'

'Then we need to head off straight away to catch them before they leave,' Alamo said. 'You ride direct to Buckskin and bring help.'

The urgency of the situation spurred both parties to action. Alamo and his buddy commandeered the horses of the two dead outlaws which had been well rested. The three riders then galloped off at full tilt down the narrow creek. At War Bonnet Rock they split up. Hasty farewells were made. Entreaties to take care aligned with tender looks passed between the young couple.

Todd offered up a silent prayer that this would not be last he saw of Freda Johnson. She disappeared in a cloud of dust, a final wave seeming to accord with her paramour's petition.

The pace of the two riders slowed as they neared the imposing bulwark of Castle Canyon. Todd Heffridge would have fully admired the magnificent edifice towering over the surrounding landscape had his mind not been on more imperative issues. Without pausing to ascertain if any guards had been posted, he pushed straight on into the dark ravine. Luck was on their side. Bremen's single-minded desire to regain the stolen map had eclipsed any caution he might otherwise have displayed. After all, this place had remained hidden for many years.

Only when they neared the amphitheatre at the end did caution take precedence. The gang were immediately spotted loading up a wagon with bags of what had to be gold nuggets.

'Looks like we arrived in the nick of time, buddy,' Streater whispered.

'Get the horses out of sight and we'll set up positions in these rocks close to the canyon entrance,' came back the tense reply. 'You on that side and me here. That way we can keep them penned in until Sheriff Bowman arrives.'

'Or until we run out of ammo,' countered the ever sceptical Kid.

'Then make every shot count,' replied his partner.

They only just managed to get in position when Bremen whipped up the wagon team and headed for the Canyon's narrow exit. He was flanked by his minions. Smiles were evident on the faces of the thieves. This had been a highly successful venture that every last one of them would profit from, especially Spider Bremen. They had every reason to be upbeat.

The lurid grins were wiped off their smug faces when the warning shot from a rifle buzzed past Bremen's head.

'That's as far as you go,' was the brusque warning from the hidden challenger. 'None of you rats is leaving here unless in chains or a pine box. Surrender now or go down in a hail of lead.'

Bremen forcibly thrust off the inertia threatening to stifle his reactions. It was that damn blasted wrangler again. The pesky varmint had somehow picked up their trail. It had to be the woman's doing. They must have got the better of Cherokee Joe and Scab Lakin and rescued her. All this flitted through his brain in a matter of seconds. The main objective now was to force a way through the Canyon.

Six against two was more than enough to cook their goose.

'Spread out, boys, and take those meddling critters down,' he ordered. 'It shouldn't take us more than a few minutes to winkle them out.' Then in a louder voice, he hollered at his assailants, 'You critters should have kept riding. Interfering in my business is gonna buy you a free plot on Boot Hill.' To emphasize his threat, he hauled off a couple of shots into the rocks guarding the Canyon's only outlet.

'You can try, mister,' Alamo replied laughingly. 'But you ain't going nowhere.'

'OK, let 'em have it, boys!' growled the incensed gang leader.

Gunfire immediately erupted. The harsh sound of bullets whining and ricocheting off the rocks echoed around the enclosed bowl. Smoke from numerous barrels filled the air with the smell of burnt powder. But the attackers had chosen their stand perfectly. Huggy Johnson had been right. He also must have been an army man, mused Kid Streater as he levered off another round.

The sudden violence within their hallowed realm forced a group of idling buzzards into a hasty flight. Circling high above the unwarranted invasion, they squawked madly. But to no effect. The battle continued, unheeding of their disapproval.

Down below, however, it soon became patently obvious to the gang boss that his conjecture of a swift defeat was premature. The assailants were dug in and there was no easy way to eject them. Yet still he urged his men to press forward while keeping his head down behind the wagon.

A careless hard case called Flint Axle was the first to bite the dust when too much of his large ungainly frame was exposed. This made the others more cautious. No threats or bribes from Bremen could persuade them to follow their sidekick's path.

And so the battle of Castle Canyon raged on. Few shots were needed by the holding force to effectively neutralize their opponents. They were too well ensconced. Which was as well owing to a lack of ammunition. Both sides now realized that a stalemate had been reached. This suited Alamo and his partner. All they had to do was await the imminent arrival of the sheriff and his posse.

A lull in the fighting saw Spider Bremen attempting his usual ploy of bribery. 'There's enough gold here for us all,' he pleaded. 'I'm willing to split fifty-fifty if'n you let us go. What do you say?'

A harsh belt of laughter greeted the offer. 'No chance, buster,' Alamo rapped. 'There's only one way you're leaving here.' A bullet clipped the side of the wagon behind which Bremen was cowering. 'The sheriff will be here soon. So you won't have long to wait.'

As if in answer to the sharp-edge threat, Clay Bowman and six rapidly sworn in deputies trundled to a halt some fifty yards back from where the two wranglers were emplaced. The sound of gunfire funnelling down the narrow ravine had given clear warning of the danger up ahead. He and his men scuttled crab-like towards the opening. Adding their firepower to that of the defenders forced Bremen's men into a hasty retreat.

The tables had been turned. Defenders were now transformed into attackers.

Bremen knew that the end was nigh. A lurid spate of irreverent curses were spat out. But the wily denizen was not finished yet. He still held an ace up his sleeve.

149

FIFTEEN

THE FLYING DUTCHMAN?

Ignoring his panic-stricken men, Bremen scrambled up onto the seat of the wagon, grabbed the leathers and slapped the team into motion. Before anybody was aware of what was happening, he had ploughed through the star-spangled interlopers. Hank Wardle and two other deputies were tossed aside like rag dolls.

Seeing his nemesis escaping galvanized Alamo into action. 'You mop up these rats, Sheriff,' he hurriedly called out, emerging from cover. 'I'm going after Bremen.' Without waiting for any response, he dashed across to his horse and hurtled off in pursuit of the runaway.

There was no way Todd could overtake the wagon in the confines of Castle Canyon. Nor could he allow himself to get too close in case the guy pulled his gun. Only when they emerged onto the open plain did the chase really hot up. Thundering across the arid sward, the team of four horses was able to substantially pick up the pace. Bremen mercilessly applied the long bull whip to urge the sweating mustangs to the limits of their endurance.

The dogged pursuer kept pace before gradually overhauling the wagon. His objective was to come up on the side and dive into the bed of the wagon. Slowly he drew level. And that was when Bremen sensed that he was not alone. He turned on the hard bench seat, mouth dropping open when he saw who was in pursuit. Was he forever going to be dogged by this spawn of the devil? A brutish scowl soured his face. He cursed aloud. But the epithet was instantly snatched away by the wind.

Alamo saw his chance and dived. Hands clawed at the sides of the bouncing wagon. But he managed to keep his balance.

Bremen knew that he had to get rid of this irritating thorn in his hide once and for all. He swung round, aiming to use the lethal whip. The angry serpent lashed across Alamo's right shoulder, coiling around his body. The pain of the harsh blow was countered by a manic desire for retribution. This guy and his minions had caused him and those whom he cared for nothing but grief.

He grabbed hold of the whip and pulled. To avoid being jerked off balance, Bremen was forced to release his hold. Alamo threw the whip aside and lunged for the gambler. Both protagonists crashed down onto the bags of gold.

Lacking the discipline administered by a competent driver, the wagon careered onward out of control. At any moment it could strike a rock and disintegrate. The imminent danger was ignored by the two fighters whose sole intent was to beat each other to a pulp.

Both were trading blows, desperate to gain the advantage. But slugging it out on a juddering wagon in the desert could not continue for long. They soon tumbled over. Luckily it was Alamo who landed on top. He gripped the gambler's shirt front and launched a couple of solid punches into the exposed visage. That did the trick. The guy's head lolled back, eyes rolling up as consciousness departed.

No time was lost by the winner of the fracas. Disaster could be moments away. Alamo scrambled onto the seat, frantically searching for the abandoned reins. He gathered them up and tugged hard, urging the terrified animals to slow down. For what seemed like a month of moons, they resisted threatening to charge onward into oblivion.

Alamo's very survival was now imperilled by the wild stampede. Desperation lent strength to his arms. He screamed out, urging the animals to show restraint. The plea appeared to have fallen on deaf ears. Then slowly but surely the frenzied dash wavered. In the nick of time, the snorting team stumbled to a hoof stomping halt on the lip of a deep arroyo. Another few feet and it would have been a long goodbye.

But no time could be allotted to regain his composure. Already Spider Bremen was showing signs of regaining his senses. Alamo quickly tied the guy up securely with a lariat before retracing his steps back to Castle Canyon.

There he found that Sheriff Bowman had the gang secured.

'When Bremen skidaddled with the loot, these guys lost the will to resist,' Bowman informed the wagon driver. 'Squint Haikon was the only one to resist. And he was shot while trying to make a break with a bag of gold.' Yet far from being jubilant at the arrests, a guilt-laden expression cloaked the sheriff's face.

Alamo picked up on the lawman's unease. 'Some'n bothering you, Sheriff?' he asked, stepping down off the wagon.

The tough law enforcer swallowed nervously. He was unused to being proved wrong. But he was man enough to admit that accusing the two wranglers of robbery and murder had been a bad error of judgement. And he was genuinely contrite. 'I'm sure sorry for doubting you, Mr Heffridge. Freda filled us in on all the details. Guess I jumped in feet first without thinking.'

Alamo accepted the apology. 'As things stood at the time, nobody could blame you for that.' But he was more concerned about Freda's welfare. 'Where is she?' he anxiously posited. 'Is she all right?'

'Don't worry,' Bowman assured him, relieved that no animosity had been harboured. 'I left her at the hotel.'

Kid Streater's thoughts were with Galloping Jane and her safety. Bowman, unfortunately, was unable to give him the same assurance.

Glad to be back in his true element and without further ado, the sheriff dragged the helpless gambler off the wagon. 'You've caused me a heap of problems, Bremen. Now I'm gonna make sure you answer for them in a court of law. Get this scumbag out of my sight.' The snarled order was for Hank Wardle who purposely made certain to add his own condemnation of the critter with a cuff to the head. The sly deputy knew where his best interests lay.

Before they headed back to Buckskin, Bowman handed Todd the money he had confiscated from his saddle bags. 'Reckon you boys have earned every last nickel of this dough. My only advice is to invest it wisely. Gambling is a mug's game.'

Alamo threw an expressive look towards his partner. 'You take heed of what the wise sheriff is telling you, Kid.' The blank response told him that the comment had struck a brick wall.

Freda Johnson's arrival in Buckskin together with the hurried gathering together of a posse had not passed unnoticed by Slickback Charlie. It was patently clear to the furtive barman that Bremen's plans had been thwarted. The boss was no longer top dog. His time had run out. And the bartender did not want to go down with him.

The only safe way to avoid any backslash was to quit town. But he needed funds for that. Always the astute operator, he was well aware that the gambler kept a secret stash of dough in a box under the floorboards of his office. Quickly he hurried upstairs and purloined the hefty wedge. There was around five grand inside. Enough to provide him with a solid grubstake.

BAD DEAL IN BUCKSKIN

Next job was to free Galloping Jane and persuade her to overlook his indiscretion with a payoff. That way nobody would come after him. What he hadn't reckoned with was the woman's refusal to be bought off. As soon as the offer was proposed, Jane laid down a smile of apparent concurrence with the odious barkeep's scheme. Then she kneed him hard in the groin, following through with a solid uppercut.

Grabbing the rat by his coat collar, she hurled him bodily into the cellar. Pure anger had given her muscles the strength of a titan.

'Think you can just pretend nothing happened, you low-life snake in the grass,' the madam railed acidly. 'Nobody treats Jane Channing like an animal and figures a few bucks will keep her quiet.'

She slammed the door on the moaning barman, sucking in lungfuls of pure clean air. After a couple of days in that hell hole, she stunk to high heaven. Her whole body was screaming for a complete sanitization. A hot bath, plenty of soothing unguents and a new set of clothes were a priority.

Sometime later Jane and Freda Johnson met up outside the National Hotel by accident. They had never previously met but soon got to talking. The realization that they were so closely linked by the unusual circumstances of recent days was a startling revelation. Both women were on tenterhooks as they awaited the return of their men. There was no guarantee that everything would turn out well.

'I'm hoping that Alamo will become a partner with me

in running the mine once it has been registered,' Freda informed her new friend.

Jane nodded. 'And I'm sure the Kid will have no reservations about helping me manage the Rim Rock. Be like a dream come true for the guy. It's about time he settled down. With me at the helm, of course.'

Freda smiled. 'Of course. I couldn't agree more.'

The arrival of the posse and their bunch of forlorn prisoners came as a huge relief, especially when the two couples were reunited. They immediately fell into each other's arms. Lingering hugs and kisses were avidly exchanged, surreptitiously accompanied by sly winks between the two ladies.

The sun was shining. It was a lovely day for new beginnings.

POSTSCRIPT

Arguably the most well-known mystery in the New World, the legend of the Lost Dutchman's mine still continues to fascinate treasure seekers from all parts of the compass. Its alleged location is somewhere within the environs of Superstition Mountain to the east of Phoenix, Arizona. Did a miner really discover a fortune in lost gold within this apocryphal region? And what strange forces have led to the unexplained disappearance of so many intrepid explorers intent on solving the enigma?

These and other questions have been posed since a Spanish conquistador first discovered a rich vein of gold here in 1845. Don Miguel Peralta memorized the location, intending to return with sufficient men to excavate the pay dirt. Meanwhile, the Apaches had grown angry at this invasion of their lands. Peralta and his men were massacred before the explorer had a chance to transport the treasure out of the area. For years afterwards, men came across remnants of the failed venture.

Most renowned of all the subsequent explorers was Jacob Weis who was not a Dutchman at all but a German immigrant. Weis worked numerous claims before he arrived in Arizona around 1870. Many stories have been told of how he came by his good fortune. Certainly Weis is known to have worked in and around the area encompassing Superstition Mountain for over twenty years. Long periods would pass with no sighting of the prospector. Then he would show up unexpectedly, shelling out for drinks with his gold nuggets. Some tried following him back into the wilderness. But the canny miner was always able to throw them off the scent.

Since that early first discovery, nobody has been able to unequivocally pinpoint the secret hoard and finally put the legend to rest. Perhaps you will have more luck. But before setting out, take heed that too many unexplained deaths have occurred over the years in pursuit of this mystifying dream.